THE COLOURS OF MAN

THE COLOURS OF MAN

Micheál Ó Conghaile (signature)

Micheál Ó Conghaile

Moccic @ gmail.com (handwritten)

Cló Iar-Chonnacht
Indreabhán
Conamara

First published 2012
© Cló Iar-Chonnacht 2012

ISBN 978-1-908947-00-0

Illustrations: Brian Bourke
Cover artwork: Nguyễn Hu'ng Trinh
Cover Deisgn: Little Bird Design

the arts council ealaíon | cistiú litríocht artscouncil.ie   Cló Iar-Chonnacht receives financial assistance from The Arts Council.

Publisher: Cló Iar-Chonnacht, Indreabhán, Co. na Gaillimhe.
Tel: 091–593307 Fax: 091–593362 e-mail: cic@iol.ie
Printing: Castle Print, Galway.

CONTENTS

Mar leacht beag cuimhneachán ar fhear mór

Mike Diskin (1962-2012)

INTRODUCTION

Brian Ó Conchubhair

Micheál Ó Conghaile, born in 1962 on Inis Treabhair, an island off the Connemara coast, is well known to Irish-language readers as an award-winning writer. His three collections of short stories, *Mac an tSagairt* (1986), *An Fear a Phléasc* (1997) and *An Fear Nach nDéanann Gáire* (2003), some of which have been translated into various languages including Albanian, Croatian, German, Macedonian, Norwegian, Polish, Romanian and Slovenian, have garnered numerous accolades.

One may legitimately ask, therefore, why Ó Conghaile would translate his work into English rather than assume a political stance on translation à la Biddy Jenkinson, Louis de Paor and Michael Hartnett? His attitude is, perhaps, informed by several factors. Ó Conghaile has argued for translating the best of Irish-language literature and contends that translation into English promotes Irish-language literature internationally by facilitating its translation into other languages. As Michael Cronin posited in the *Irish Times* (7 April 2001): 'no matter how often a book is praised, the praise is meaningless for English-language readers without Irish until they can read the text in translation.' Fundamental also, perhaps, is Ó Conghaile's experience of submitting 'Athair' to the *Sunday Tribune*. The story lingered, receiving neither acknowledgement nor acceptance until a year later when Ó Conghaile serendipitously submitted 'Father', its English-language translation. Published and placed on the *Tribune*'s shortlist for story of the year, it subsequently won the competition outright and earned Ó Conghaile the prestigious Hennessy Writer of the Year Award. Recognition is important for authors and few authors are willing for their works, however pure or serene, to blush unseen in dark, unfathomed caves of Irish-language journals or on the bottom shelves of bookshops.

Ó Conghaile's decision to write in Irish is neither politically motivated nor culturally charged. He writes in Irish not for love of the language but because it is his first language – the language in which he best creates. Were he more comfortable writing in English, that would be his medium of choice. He never envisions himself writing in English, but is nevertheless happy to have his work translated:

> Dá mbeinn níos fearr ag scríobh i mBéarla, scríobhfainn i mBéarla le bheith fírinneach. Ní le grá teanga atá mise ag scríobh i nGaeilge ach le grá don ealaíon atá idir lámha agam. Ní bheinn ar mo shuaimhneas ag scríobh i mBéarla … Ní fheicim mé féin ag scríobh i mBéarla go deo ach ba bhreá liom dá n-aistreofaí an chuid is fearr dá bhfuil scríofa agam agus go mbeadh fáil níos leithne air.

[Were I better at writing in English, I would write in English, to be truthful. I don't write in Irish for love of the language but for love of the art I'm engaged in. I wouldn't be at ease writing in English ... I never see myself writing in English but I would like if the best of what I have written were translated and more widely available.]

This urge has as much to do with attracting and enticing readers as it has with recognition. Writers write to be read, not to be admired for cultural nationalist principles or praised for principled linguistic stances. Writers pine for responses, for connection from readers. The urge to be translated is a need to expand the potential readership and render the labour of love accessible to as broad, as wide and as diverse an audience of readers as possible. It is in essence a democratic urge to share, commune and connect; to engage with a broader and wider spectrum and enter the light of other languages and cultures.

Ó Conghaile's use of language is contemporary, uncluttered and comfortable in its own skin. In keeping with the thematic consistency of these stories, there is here an embrace and celebration of the demotic, the natural spoken vernacular, rather than a kowtowing to some idealised petrified form of language. If the scenes are at times fantastical, the language is always grounded and playful, honest and true, yet keenly aware of, and alert to, its own hidden meanings and metaphorical potential. *Mac an tSagairt*, his first collection, stirred controversy not only for its thematic focus on abortion, suicide, marital break-up, expulsion from home and children born out of wedlock, but for its then sensational use of colloquial Irish, heavily laced with English borrowings, international cognates and Anglo-American syntax. Subsequently Ó Conghaile explained in an interview in the *Canadian Journal of Irish Studies* (2005, 56) that his objective was:

> to capture the contemporary language of the characters in the *Gaeltacht* [Irish-speaking area] I was writing about. I suppose as a writer that is the best thing I brought with me from my home and from being an Irish speaker. An ear for the spoken language ... or I should say languages as there are different levels of the Irish language spoken in the *Gaeltacht* ... Normally, when writing conversation, I would stick to that and that might mean mixing some words or phrases in English in through the Irish. There are times when the word in English is a lot stronger than the word in Irish. It can hit a lot harder. If the English word is used in the *Gaeltacht* it has a stronger register for me as a reader and a writer than the Irish translation ...

In relation to his successful translations of Martin McDonagh's plays and the incorporation of a similar linguistic strategy, he rationalised his approach in a lecture at the 2012 American Conference for Irish Studies in New Orleans as follows:

> Bhí na focail Bhéarla i bhfad níos láidre, níos cumhachtaí agus bhí níos mó fórsa ag baint leo – rud a bhí an-soiléir domsa ón gcaoi ar ghlac an lucht éisteachta san amharclann leo. Glacaim leis gur bochtú ar an teanga – an Ghaeilge – é focail dá leithéid a úsáid ach is saibhriú ar an dráma, ar an léiriú, é – agus b'in an phríomhaidhm sa gcás seo. Go deimhin b'in an dualgas a leag mé orm féin ... An

chúis ná go bhfuil na focail Bhéarla úd níos cumhachtaí, níos scanrúla agus níos pianmhara ná na haistriúcháin Ghaeilge i síce an chainteora Gaeltachta.
[The English words were stronger and more powerful – something that was very clear to me from the way the theatre audience reacted to them. I concede that the use of such words is a degradation of the language – Irish – but it is a bonus for the play, for the production, and that is the objective here. Indeed that is how I tasked myself ... The reason is that those English words are more powerful, more intimidating and more painful for the Gaeltacht-speaker's psyche.]

This metalingual aspect, more often than not, is lost in translation. The hues and shades of competing languages, diglossic exchanges and the hidden linguistic and cultural history they betray are homogenised and standardised when translated. The metalingual back and forth and the code switching from the acrolect to the basilect, a key trait of Ó Conghaile's work, is as much a reflection of the community's personality as it is the author's creation, and gives an immediate and distinct style and location to the stories in the original. The minute gradations and imbalances are flattened; the interplay and chemistry between English, Irish, Hiberno-Irish and Mid-Atlantic-global-*inglish* are shredded in the linguistic blender, and English, as the dominant flavour, overpowers the delicate tastes, resulting in a powerful but less sophisticated linguistic palate. Such is the cost of translation. Narrative structure and thematic coherence may be maintained, but linguistic and stylistic integrity and interplay are often lost in the processed product. The translators here have embraced different styles to re-create the strangeness and quirkiness of the original, but the task they faced was herculean given the linguistic constraints: reproducing a sophisticated cocktail using only one ingredient.

Ó Conghaile practises different genres but also embraces different styles – as Alan Titley observed in an early review in *Comhar* entitled 'An bobailín á scaoileadh amach' (December, 1987). Regardless of styles – realist, magic realist, postmodern or social realist – a compelling artistic and articulate use of language is constant. If best known for the fantastical, postmodern, non-realist stories (some of which appear in the 2001 collection *Twisted Truths*) chronicling incredible events, unlikely happenings and bizarre acts – often grotesque and unbelievable – such as many of the stories in *An Fear a Phléasc* and *An Fear nach nDéanann Gáire* – he is also adept at classical realism. *Mac an tSagairt*'s honest and realistic depiction of rape, suicide and abortion generated controversy – referred to in the 2005 interview mentioned above. In more recent collections, readers find additional realist stories such as the award-winning 'Father', 'Lost in Connemara' and 'The Book of Sin' competing with magic realist and postmodern stories such as 'The Man Who Exploded', 'Seven Hundred Watches' and 'No Room in Heaven'. In his realistic stories Ó Conghaile depicts contemporary Ireland, specifically contemporary Connemara, at moments of intense emotional crisis: cancer, suicide, coming out, final moments before (and after) death. These touching and tender stories contrast with the verbal energy and black humour of his postmodern stories but speak to the varying styles and techniques evident in his three collections to date, and the story 'No Room in Heaven', from a forthcoming collection entitled *An Fear ar Ball*, suggests yet another stylistic string to his bow, an evolution that speaks to an engagement and re-imagining of folkloric narratives.

The dazzling colours of this collection laugh aloud and shout to us to join them in their riotous travels and call on us to reflect on moments of profound loss, serious challenges and deep fears. The tone, however, is reformist rather than revolutionary with change a constant factor, be it in 'The Rock', 'The Book of Sin' or 'Father'. The old master narratives (truth, chronology, morality) are surely and steadily destabilised and undermined in stories such as 'The Man Who Exploded' and 'The Man Who Never Laughs'. Yet in such stories that challenge and reject standard religious dogma and institutional authority, there is nevertheless a very strong sense of spirituality and wonder, and an equally strong concern with issues of forgiveness, repentance and mercy. The shock and aftermath of loss and the emotional human void left in the wake of deep personal injury is a recurring theme in all of Ó Conghaile's work and no less so in these stories. And many of the finest compositions are those realist stories that tackle visceral emotive questions with searing honesty. The question of how to respond to emotional crisis is a frequent trope in his realist stories. As the character in 'Father' says, 'A deadly silence is unworkable, impossible, as long, drawn-out and painful as a birth.' When such questions are answered, they elicit black humour in many of his postmodern and non-realist stories – which establishes a binary between the realist and non-realist stories. Stories such as 'The Mercyfucker', 'The Colours of Man', 'Father', 'Junctions' and 'Lost in Connemara' speak to transformation, loss, empathy, risk and truth. These stories tackle serious social issues that often emerge from broken and deeply flawed institutions and cultural practices. In several instances the trauma is exacerbated by mainstream culture's failure to recognise the existence of these 'illicit' and 'unofficial' relationships and their subsequent loss. Inherent in these stories is a subtle condemnation of greed, commercialisation and all-encompassing doctrines – be they moral, commercial, political or environmental crusades – that fail to recognise or accommodate human desires, failings and frailties. If there is a recurring motif in these stories, diverse in terms of themes, style and tone, it is the recurring chorus that living rather than life is sacred, a là Hazlitt's 'On the Love of Life'. Extracting the maximum from life and time is a repeated trope, particularly in 'At the Station' which stands in direct contrast to 'The Rock' and 'Whatever I Liked' where the character claims in court that he is guilty only of 'being alive'. These stories do not celebrate the oppressed or marginalised; to do so would reduce them to polemic. Although the stories have been welcomed by the gay community, they recognise and acknowledge submerged populations, and rather than apotheosise them, show them at their most vulnerable and weakest – under attack, grieving, recoiling, retreating, struggling to survive. This pluralistic collection celebrates the profusion of all the colours of man and all the shades, hues and tones of the spectrum contained within man and humankind. These colourful stories tell of people who cry out for understanding and shelter and who plead for permission and the right to live according to their needs and desires rather than abide by strictures and arbitrary codes that refuse to acknowledge or accommodate them. This collection of seventeen stories, encompassing stories from a twenty-six-year period of writing, demonstrates not only a variety of styles, both literary and linguistic, but a deftness of style that characterises Ó Conghaile's stories and marks him among the most accomplished and distinctive short story writers of his generation writing in either English or Irish in Ireland. His work to date has found homes in various European languages; it is both fitting and timely, therefore, that a collection of his finest work should now be available to readers of English in a single volume.

THE COLOURS OF MAN

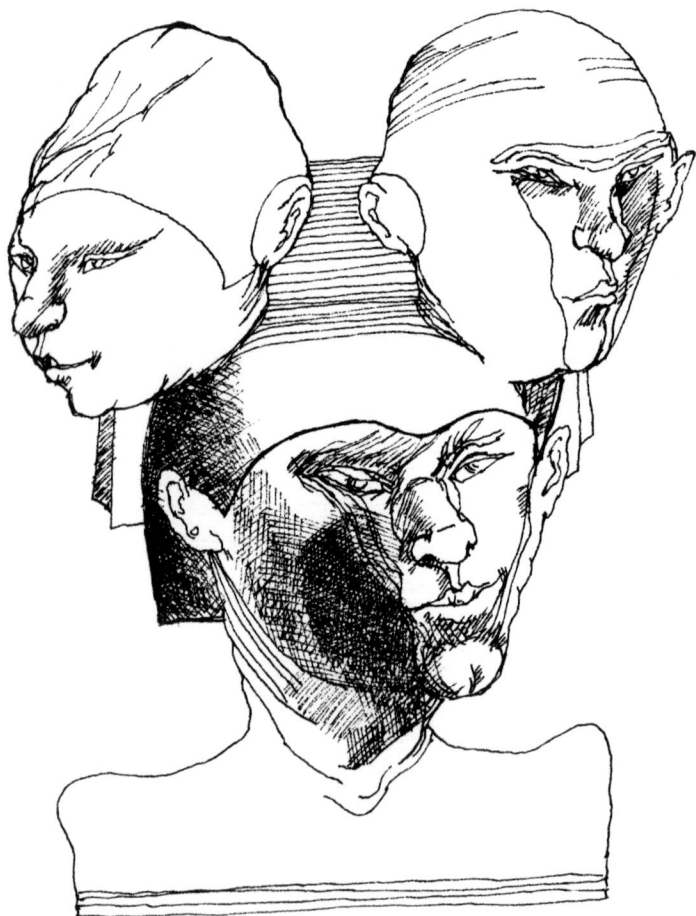

I was with him that night. Indeed, I was the last person to see him, bolting the gate from the inside. He was wearing a red polo neck, blue jeans, and a scarf the colours of Man United.

I thought he was in great spirits that night. We started off in Greens. Couldn't say exactly what time. It was well after seven, maybe nearer eight. You have to go out early on Sunday nights. You have to have an early start, he used to say, cursing the pubs. Ten o'clock was no hour to be closing, not at all. Not that he would drink an awful lot; he liked a few pints, that's all. Craving for a drink wasn't what brought him to the pubs.

He had four pints that night. I'm sure he had no more. He was only out for the company, like myself. The fun. The lads. Meeting people, that's what he wanted. I don't think I ever saw him stuck to a seat in a pub. He'd normally be standing at the counter, gabbing away. He'd stop people going by and pick on them, or pretend to, or ask them about something. They'd talk of drink, dances, football, women. He'd an eye for the ladies, like myself. What's the harm in that? A young lad. He would have been twenty-one next autumn. I don't think he was going steady with anyone at the time. I'd have known. Pauline had left him a long while ago, coming and going. Róisín, he dropped. She was no good, he said. None of us had a woman with us that night.

There was nothing cooking in Greens. We went off to

Doody's. It was coming up to nine. The music was great, but we were packed like sardines. We stayed there until closing time. It was good crack. We spent most of the night with the lads. Sussed the place out a few times, but got nothing. Bit of skirt there all right, talkative and lively among themselves, until you'd say something to them. We tried our best with them, but it was useless. They'd too many excuses. Didn't want to dance. Had boyfriends of their own. Had no interest in us. They were in company. Most of them looked at us brazenly, sour-faced. All we were after, in the heel of the hunt, was sex, or so they seemed to be telling us. We didn't care.

We finished at the disco. We didn't leave the corner of the hall until we'd demolished a six-pack one of the lads had brought in under his coat. The place was packed. We spent the rest of the night on the scent. 'How ya, how's it going?' We elbowed our way into groups. Circular groups knitted together. We weren't always welcome. They didn't need us. Too busy whispering, acting the fool, repeating stories.

We moved about. Spoke to a lot of people. Got the odd dance too. I remember he danced his heart out. He'd always liked a bit of footwork and that night was no different. As I said, he hadn't much taken and he had his wits about him. He danced to all types of music and fairly shook the floor. The Boomtown Rats had the most effect on him: 'I Don't Like Mondays'. He liked the music, the movements, and he moved with them. He would sing the words with gusto. Knew them all. I was out dancing too. You'd think by the end of the night that he hadn't got much out of it; or maybe I'm just thinking that now.

'We didn't do too good,' I said, ragging him a bit. 'Not a skirt or even a hem.'

He lit a fag. Inhaled deeply. A tunnel of smoke came from his rounded mouth.

'Says who? What put it in your head it was a woman I was after?'

That stopped me in my tracks. For a second it wasn't him that was there at all. Somehow it wasn't him, but then it was again.

I made little of the outburst. 'You wouldn't say that now if you had an armful of one, or if you were saddling one up for yourself after the first whiff.'

He pretended not to react, but I saw signs of a smile on his mouth. He took another drag. Suddenly he burst out laughing. It was after one o'clock by then.

We spent about another hour hovering around outside. Someone took off to the chipper and came back with burgers and chips. We were messing around, lighting up, blathering and arguing about women. In praise, in blame, and, sometimes, in judgement. The Sunday match was talked about. The team was blamed; the referee damned. We talked about powerful motorbikes; Suzukis were praised and others. The great big cars we would like to drive some day if we won the Lotto. The Subarus and the BMWs that the joyriders in Dublin go for. We cracked a few jokes. Some of them foul.

Someone mentioned the casinos. We'll go. It's too early to go home. Who'd want to go home this early? Would we go or not? What's the point? What's the point going home? We have to go somewhere. Eventually a gang of them went there. Everybody, except the two of us, myself and himself.

We went straight home. I asked him into the house for a while; it was fast approaching three o'clock. I knew the old folks would be asleep and we'd have the place to ourselves.

In we go. I plugged in the kettle. Put out an ashtray. Took down the coffee and biscuits. Two hours we spent talking, about this and that, at our leisure.

We'd been to the same school and we talked about it. We'd left the same year. Dole after that. Often doing nothing. Quiet during the week and out at the weekends. Sleeping it off in the mornings. Doing the odd little job, here and there. Half thinking of going to England. Never did. Stuck around Galway. The odd trip to Dublin. He'd often say, actually, that he would like to live there. That was one of his plans. We talked about the girls we had ... the type of woman we'd like to settle down with someday ... films we enjoyed ... countries we'd visit ... the type of work we'd like to get. Work that would bring us money and bring meaning to our lives.

He'd stay until morning, you'd imagine, if I could keep up with him. No sign of sleep at all on him. From watching him and listening to him, you'd think he was only coming into his own. At last, whether I liked it or not, my eyes began to close and I conked out on the sofa.

'Wake up!' he said rudely, giving me a good shake. He stubbed out a butt in the ashtray. 'It's time I went home.'

I roused myself. It was making for five a.m. He wrapped his scarf around his neck. I was only thinking of sleep, exhausted. Strange, though, that I should walk out with him, and his people's house only a couple of hundred yards down the road. Maybe it was just to fill my lungs with fresh air before sleeping, to sharpen up a bit? Anyway, I went out with him.

Down the road we go, in the faintly brightening morning. That walk, that time of the night, I often remember now, as though a spirit were following me, a ghost. It was chilly. No light shone from any house. He didn't say a word along the way. I often thought since then that I would have been happy had he spoke – about anything – so that I would remember that journey. We stood at the gate a mere moment. All I wanted – and I hate saying it now – was to hurry off home out of the cold.

A sharp knock on my bedroom door woke me. It was only seven. It was my mother – to break the bad news. News that left me frozen, lifeless in the bed for a long while. Who'd ever think it? What a weak and miserable little bird was this world, the way you could change it so drastically with the flick of a wrist.

What had he been bottling up all this time? Now, suddenly, I had a thousand questions to ask him. Wasn't I in the same boat as him? That's what I wanted to say. What a pity he hadn't told me of this plan, if he had it planned at all; I was his best friend. He played a trick on me and he won. In a way, it was easy to blame him. I remember now, I felt nausea and even anger. I didn't know rightly what to do.

I didn't go to the funeral at all. I couldn't. I took one single look at him in the coffin, that's all. I wanted to die myself. It was worth dying. We might be together again, the two of us and, if not, could it be any worse than now?

I was brought up to the graveyard some days later. They thought it might help me; that I'd have to go early or it would get worse with the passing of time. I could spend my whole life and never go there.

It taught me a lot. I understood things properly, I think, for the first time. Life was over, for ever. Football matches were over ... hanging around street corners ... winking at the girls ... all the plans we had ever made.

I won't visit the grave ever again, I'd say. It's safer that way. The grave's teeth are sharp; they've gone through me already. No, that's not how it should be. That's not how I want to remember him. I'd prefer to remember him young, full of fun, twenty years old, bursting with vigour, free and easy. And the two of us planning something new.

I visited his people that evening. I thought it best to get it over with. They were welcoming and friendly. Considerate. We drank a cup of coffee together. Coffee and biscuits. We were very nice to each other. The most difficult part, for me, was to know what to talk about. I spoke about him. They spoke about me, about themselves, about life, even about the weather, about everything. I decided not to go near them again for a good while.

I prefer now not to bring it up in conversation. I talk to myself about it a lot. Asking myself and tormenting myself. I haven't started answering myself properly yet. Maybe that's the way it suits him? That's why, maybe, he never told me anything. I'm the best friend he ever had, you see. He respected me too, I'm sure of that.

Do you know, sometimes when I stroll downtown I half expect to see him. He'll come loping around some street corner, his hands sunk deep in his pockets, keenly gazing at the world around him, whistling brightly the latest tune in the charts.

And I was with him that night. Indeed, in a strange way I'm happy that it was me who last set eyes on him ... bolting the gate from the inside. He wore a red polo neck. A red polo neck, old blue jeans, and a scarf the colours of man.

Translated by Gabriel Rosenstock

DEATH AT A FUNERAL

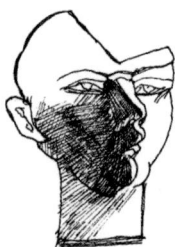

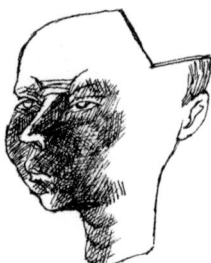

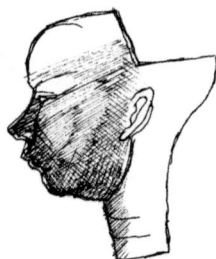

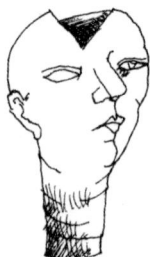

It would have been ridiculous for Eamon Bartley to stay ensconced in his coffin any longer. He couldn't anyway. He was far too good to have died. Every one of the merry mourners at the funeral were praising him – praising him up and down and back to front and top to bottom and arse to elbow – even those who hated his guts once upon a time; those who had it in for him due to some old dispute; those who cursed him roundly and fucked him from a height; those who hadn't talked to him for yonks; those who crossed the road to avoid him, or looked right when he was on the left, or who stared at the ground if he was all around them. Every man jack of them praising him with gusto now. They were mourning him and mourning him and mourning him, they sure were.

'Eamon was all right you know, the poor fucker.'

'The whole town will miss him.'

'You could depend on Eamon, a sound man.'

'The poor soul, God love him.'

'He was kind and helpful to everybody.'

'He was all of that and more, even if he wasn't the full shilling.'

'Too true.'

'You never said a more honest word.'

'Absolutely.'

Eamon suddenly began to think that he'd be a proper fool to remain dead in his coffin any longer. Not one minute longer. Neither right nor proper nor appropriate. Besides it would be wrong to these good, heartbroken people gathered around him. Maybe I'm confused, he thought to himself, or maybe I'm not the same person I was ... in which case it wasn't me who knocked up Micil Bawn's young one at all; or broke into Mary Andy's shop and made off with two thousand euros, or nicked the sugar lumps from the priest's tea the day he was around for the stations, or who crashed into Martin More's nice new car without tax or insurance, or who fire-bombed the co-op's offices when they sacked me, or who broke into the police station looking for my hooch which the bastards swiped ...

With one vicious smash he crashed up through the brown coffin lid. Sat up. Straightened himself as straight as a bamboo cane in a teacher's hand.

The mourners woke up in consternation from muttering their prayers. Some of them jumped out of their skins, and into others'. A few of them gawped. Others seemed to run off in four directions at once, as if they were doing a set-dance mixed up with a waltz. The rest of them froze like icicles on a cold March day.

Eamon Bartley Coolan looked around him. And then looked slowly around him again in silence from person to person. His head and shoulders were barely up over the edge of the grave. He was grinning all over. A grin that grew until it went from ear to ear. A big, broad, stupid crescent grin.

'Aren't you all happy that I'm alive and kicking again?'

he said, buddy-like and upbeat. Then he stopped, expecting someone to say something, anything, even a stutter. But there was no answer, not a word. He broke the silence again.

'Look, even though I liked the other life better than this miserable vale of tears, I just couldn't not come back, you missed me so much. You are all so nice, so straight. Too straight and honest really. I was really touched the way you all said nice things about me, praising me to the skies. Every single one of you. And I felt such pity for you. Your wailing and weeping would make the stones themselves burst into tears, and that's why I, that's why … Hold on a minute! Is something wrong? Why are you all so quiet, gawking at me with your big wide eyes? Do I detect some misgivings now that I've thrown away the shroud? I mean, come on, it's a bit early for me to die again, isn't it? Begging your pardon then, my friends and companions and brothers in Christ, but am I allowed to stay just a little bit longer, to live just a little bit more? Am I?'

Nobody answered him at first. Nobody spoke. They stood around like statues, like telephone poles, like stiffened stalagmites. The priest. The undertaker. The doctor. The workers. His widow. The local petty politician who turned up at every funeral with his limp handshake. Relations of all kinds. Some who had never been heard of, others who denied having anything to do with him. Toddlers and raggy urchins. Teenagers. Neighbours. People from the town. From the hills. The odd person that nobody knew …

'I drank fifteen pints at his wake. I'm telling you. Fifteen bloody pints. I never sank my moustache into so many creamy pints, the very best of pints, for the sake of a scrounger who never spent one cent on a drink in his life, nor on anything else either until he died. Don't let him spoil our day's boozing now. Believe me, he doesn't deserve to live ...'

'I was certain he was dead. Absolutely sure. Didn't I feel his pulse? I put my hand on his pulse three or four times, and I felt his heart, his ... No sign of life whatsoever. One hundred per cent sure. I'd be able to recognise a dead man rather than a live one any day before anyone else ... I have years of practice ... Think of my reputation, my good name, my professional record. I'm telling you, he doesn't deserve to live ...'

'The coffin is ruined now anyway. Whoever heard of a second-hand coffin? And it smells. His name and date of death finely and clearly engraved on its brass plate, all arrangements on the news and in the papers. It's not as if it could be used again. You couldn't flog a pine overcoat that somebody had already worn. It would be unlucky, unhealthy. Think of the risk. Even a live person wouldn't be happy to sit in a second-hand coffin ... never mind a second-corpse coffin ... never mind a dead person. For God's sake, he doesn't deserve to live ...'

'He never voted for me. Never. Not once. The Bartleys always stuck with the other crowd, they didn't change over when others did the time of that bother about the potholes and the water. When I think of all the cars we sent to bring him to the polling booth on election day. Total waste of time. Election after election. And he never once voted for me, after all I did for him. And I don't suppose he's going to change his mind now with another election coming. On mature reflection, he doesn't deserve to live ...'

'He was a nasty bastard anyway. Frightening the shite out of me on the road coming home from school. Trying to scare me. Acting the eejit. Talking about ghosts, and hobgoblins, and fairies, all those silly things that aren't there anymore. Telling stupid stories. Acting the real prick. He bullied me often enough. I used to dirty the bed, not sleep at night, and have nightmares because of him. When you think about it, he doesn't deserve to live ...'

'I put twenty euros offering on his altar. Twenty euros, boy, I did, I'm telling you. I sweated blood and tears for those twenty euros, and yet I gladly offered them up to the Divine Lord because he answered my prayers ... that I wouldn't see him sneaking past my door ever again. He was a right one ... and may God grant that he never comes snooping around again. If I had to offer another twenty euros on his altar I'd be completely bust. No way! If you ask me, he doesn't deserve to live ...'

'He was a liar. A consummate, irredeemable liar. Pretending he had snuffed it. Making fools of people. Drawing attention to himself. Throwing shapes. Acting the big cheese. Trying to show the world that we in this town are only stupid pig-ignorant blubber-brains. Well, he has another thing coming. He doesn't deserve to live ...'

'I came all of seventy miles to be here at his funeral. Seventy long Irish miles, neither give nor take an inch or a half-inch. My health isn't good, you know. I'm ailing myself. I've put my life in danger by coming all the way here just to see him laid out. So I could see him stone dead before my very own eyes. I just had to. Okay, so I had a face on me and we weren't talking for a long time, but I wouldn't give him the satisfaction of not coming to his funeral. Seventy miles, despite my bad health ... my rheumatism, varicose veins, blood pressure, weak heart ... despite my ... Ah, what the hell, he doesn't deserve to live ...'

'I'd put a bet on with the bookie. Quite simple really. Five thousand euros. Five thousand euros that he wouldn't make it to the end of the week. Jaysus, I'd lose everything. My house, my car, my ex-wife, the whole bleeding lot. Keep the final curtain down until next week and I'll have claimed my money, and I'll have made it sing. No doubt about it, he doesn't deserve to live ...'

'It's not him at all. It's some kind of evil spirit, some kind of malevolent changeling that causes havoc if it doesn't get its own way. It's not of this world at all, I'm more than certain of that. How do we know that it's not the devil incarnate in some kind of disguise? The spawn of Satan. He was always an Antichrist. He hasn't come back for our good, I'll tell you that. He doesn't deserve to live ...'

'Pretending all the time that he was a bit simple. A bit gaga. Nobody at home, like. I suppose he thinks now we believe he was so simple that he couldn't tell he should stay pegged out the way he was, like any decent corpse with a wisp of sense. Like any decent corpse with any respect for the unfortunate creatures he'd left behind. Himself and his stupid, inane, asshole simplicity. A bad, bastardy, ball-brained bollix. Let's be fair, he doesn't deserve to live ...'

'I'll never get the widow's pension now. Fat chance as long as that fat turd is around. I'll be disgraced and mortified again, like the last time when he shagged off and they called me the "live man's widow". We can't let him get away with it again. It would be appalling, unjust. He's a cheating lying deceiver anyway – letting on he was dead, the little shite. That was below the belt. The lying scumbag. He got his just desserts. If he crapped out as cold meat, let him stay crapped out to push up daisies like any half-decent man. It's bad enough when someone is a sly chancer in this life, but when they come back from the dead to be a sly chancer again, it's ten times worse. We've yapped on long enough about him. He doesn't deserve to live ...'

'I got to him just in time. Just in time to anoint him. I wouldn't have, of course, if I hadn't left my fine dinner to go cold on me. I certainly wouldn't. And he wouldn't have made his last sincere confession if it hadn't been for me. A true and genuine confession from the bottom of his heart ... real soul-searching stuff. When he was fading away and his breath coming in short wheezy gasps, I said the Act of Contrition right into his ear. I did, I did that. And before my prayer could go through his thick head and out through the other ear – puff! – he popped off. Croaked. Out for the last count. But it didn't matter, I had forgiven him all his sins, even the very worst of them, every single one of them – and I can tell you they were many and varied ... robbery, calumny, lies, cursing and swearing, blasphemy, lechery and whoring and whoring and lechering. Not to mention all the newfangled sins he had deliberately learned from the New Catechism. I'd be here until morning or beyond. By the time I was finished with him he was ready to go; as ready and as steady as a strong stone bridge, and maybe he was halfway across it on his journey to paradise if the fool had only kept going. The next time, yes, the next time, the unfortunate man may not be half as prepared. Maybe he'd be caught off-guard, on the hop. And as regards the altar offerings, they were the biggest that I have ever seen for a deceased man in this diocese. He must have been held in the greatest respect, or the greatest disrespect as the case may be, and people were relieved to see him gone. All those tenners, and twenties, and even a few fifties – and the mass cards! Hundreds of them with a tenner stuck in them all. Enough money for half the devils in hell to buy their ticket to heaven. I'd never be able to give them all back, never. I've already booked two fortnights in Bangkok, put a fat deposit on a new car. And why not? An extension wouldn't be good for him anyway. More time would be bad news. I'm only for his own good. His soul was as pure and as scrubbed clean as the new marble on a memorial monument. He wouldn't be half as ready the next time – that is, if there is to be a next time. He couldn't possibly be as prepared as he was, or his soul as ready to meet his Maker. I mean, if I was to be called out again to anoint him, I couldn't really be expected to ... I mean, how could I believe that kind of a call. Once bitten twice shy and all that. He'd be the worse for it, he'd be the one to suffer. Another sackload of sins accumulated, one blacker than the other. God's will be done. We're only for his own good. In the name of God and of His Blessed Mother, and for all our sakes and the sake of all the saints and the suffering holy souls in purgatory who are in torment, but most of all for his own sake, I have to say to you ... that ... he doesn't deserve to live ...'

'He doesn't deserve to live ...'

'Do away with him ...'

'Send him back to where he came from ...'

'Finish the job ...'

'Good riddance ...'

'For once and for all ...'

'For ever and ever ...'

'Amen.'

They beat his legs. Broke his bones. Twisted his arms.

Tortured his limbs. Split his skull in two places. They smeared blood on his face, on every part of him. Tore out his hair. Ripped out one of his balls. Bruised him black and blue with their boots and kicking. Stabbed him with knives, stabbed him anywhere they could find unstabbed flesh. Children spat and snotted at him ...

Then they blessed the body.

Translated by Alan Titley

FATHER

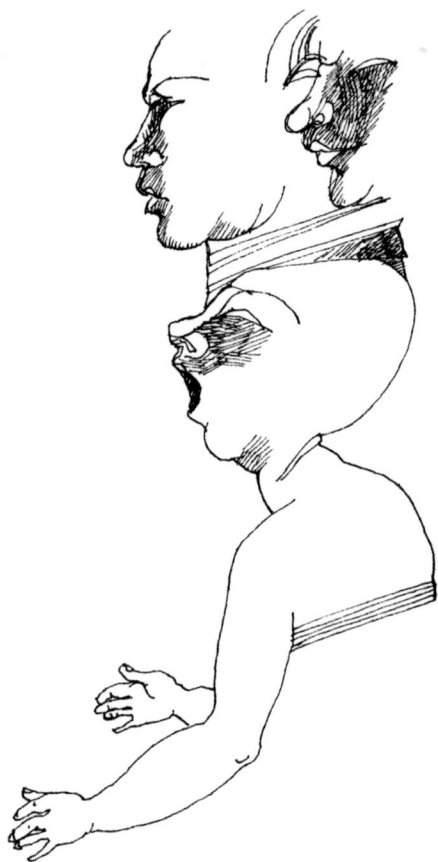

Once I had told him how was I supposed to know what to do? I had never seen my father crying before. Never. Even when Mum died nine months ago in the accident he never cried, as far as I know. I'm sure of it because it was me who brought him the bad news. And I was there the whole time, right up to the funeral, and afterwards. It was my job to stay with him. My uncles made all the arrangements, shouldered the coffin. And the neighbours, instructed by my sisters, kept the house in some order. But there was a sort of an understanding – unspoken, mind you – that it was best if I stay with Dad since I was the youngest, the only one still at home all year round.

That's how I'm nearly sure that he never shed a tear. Not in broad daylight anyway. He didn't even need his hanky, unless it was to blow his nose. Sure, he was all over the place. You could hardly get a word out of him. Long silences would go by while he just stared into the fire or out the kitchen window. But there were no tears. Maybe it was the shock. The terrible shock to his system. But then again, you wouldn't really associate tears or crying with someone like my father.

That's why I was so taken aback. Mortified. Not just the crying. But the way he cried. In fact, you couldn't really call it crying. It was more like something between a groan and a

sob stuck deep in his throat. A muffled, pained sigh of
revulsion, or so it sounded. It only lasted a few moments.
And from the way he stopped so suddenly, you would think
that he had swallowed it down like a big foul-tasting pill you
have to take on doctor's orders. He didn't even look at me,
except for a stray watery glance that skirred by when I told
him. Afterwards, it was like he was trying to hide his face
away, or half-away, from me. It should've been easier for him
somehow, but not for me; there was no way I could look him
in the face, for all I wanted to. So, while he dithered about,
I sat there like a statue, with nothing left in me but my body
heat. The breath was knocked out of both of us. Then I
realised that even his smothered cry – if cry it was – was
better than this silence. You could try to do something,
maybe, about a cry, if it was out there. But a deadly silence
was abstract and threatening. As long, drawn-out and
painful as a birth. But of what? I just felt that, throughout
the whole time, he couldn't bring himself to look at me, even
when he had recovered enough to take two deep breaths one
after the other and, finally, to string two words together.

'So you are ...' he said, as if the word stuck or swelled
up in his throat until he didn't know if it was safe to release
it, or else he hoped, perhaps, that I would say it – the word
that had clogged his ears just now, a word he was never likely
to form in his countryman's throat unless it was spat out in
some smutty joke for the lads down the pub. A word there
wasn't even a respectful word for in Irish, certainly not one
that sprang to mind ... Too busy trying to gauge his mind, I
forgot that I hadn't answered him yet when suddenly he
repeated:

'Are you telling me you're ...'

'Yes,' I said, half-consciously interrupting him with a reticence similar to his, unsure whether he was going to finish his sentence this time, or not.

'Yes,' I repeated quickly, as though the word might run and hide from me, trying for a second to make up for the empty silence.

'God save us,' he said. 'Holy Son of God *save* us.' The words came out as though he'd had to drag them one by one from Mexico. It seemed for a moment like he would have said more, something at least, if there had been a ready-made answer or platitude handy, some string of words to pluck from the silence.

'See that now,' he groaned, taking a deep sniff of the kitchen air and blowing it out again with force. 'Do you see that now?'

He grabbed the coal bucket and opened the range to top up the fire. Then he lifted a couple of sods of turf out of the 10–10–20 plastic bag beside the range and, breaking the last two bits in half over his knee to build up his corner of the crammed space of the open range, shoved them in on top. It was a habit of his to combine the coal and turf like that. The coal was too hot – and too dear to use by itself anyway, he would say – plus it was hard to burn the turf sometimes, or to get much heat out of it, especially if it was still a bit soggy after a bad summer. He took the handbrush off the hook and swept any powdery bits of turf on the range into the fire. Then he slid the iron lid back into place with a clatter and took another deep breath, focusing on the range.

'And have you told your sisters about this?'

'Yes. When they were home this summer. The night before they went back to England.'

He stopped a moment, still half-stooped over the range. He opened his mouth, then closed it again, making no sound, like a goldfish in a bowl. He tried again and, still choked with emotion, managed a broken sentence:

'And your mother – did she know?'

'Dunno,' I said. 'Mothers know a lot more than they get told.'

'Oh, they do, they do … God bless the souls of the dead.' He blessed himself, awkwardly. 'But fathers know nothing. Nothing until it's spelt out for them.'

He was standing at the table now, having poured a drop of well-water from the bucket into the kettle, which was already full. Then he placed the kettle back on the range as if he was boiling water for tea the way he did after milking-time. He always made tea with well-water, boiling it in the old kettle, instead of using tap-water and the electric kettle, unless it was early in the morning when he had no time. It would save on the electric, he always said. Even Mum couldn't get him to change. She wanted rid of the range altogether since the electric cooker was more reliable, more precise, as she used to say, for everything – boiling, baking, cooking dinners and heating up milk for the calves. 'But what if there's a power cut?' he used to say, 'due to a storm or lightning? If the electric runs out, that range will come in handy.' And any time it happened, he would turn to us, delighted, and say: 'Aren't you glad now of the old range?'

He lifted the poker, opened the top door of the range, and plunged the poker in to stir up the fire, trying to draw some flames from the depths. When the embers didn't respond very well, he turned the knob at the top of the range somewhat clumsily, making the chimney suck up the flame.

He poked the fire another couple of times, a bit deeper, trying to let the air through. Soon there were flames dancing, blue and red, licking the dark sods and fizzing and flitting over the hard coal, shyly at first but growing in courage and strength. He closed the door with a deep thud, turning the knob firmly with his left hand, and put the poker back in the corner.

'And what about Jimí Beag's daughter Síle?' he asked suddenly, as if surprised he hadn't thought of this earlier. 'Weren't you going out with her a few years ago?' he said, a hint of hope rising in his voice.

'Yes ... sort of,' I stammered. I knew it was no answer, but it was the best I could do just then.

'Sort of,' he repeated. 'What do you mean *sort of*? You either were or you weren't. Wasn't she coming round here for a year and God knows how long before that? Sure, she left Tomáisín Tom Mhary to go out with you, didn't she?' He stared at the bars over the range.

'But I was only –' changing my mind, I said, '– only eighteen back then. Nobody knows what they want at that age,' I added, 'or what's destined for them.'

'But they do at twenty-two, it seems! They think they know it all at twenty-two.'

'I'm afraid it's not that simple,' I said, surprising myself at going so far.

'Sure, it's not simple. Anything but!'

He pushed the kettle aside and opened the top of the range again as if he was checking to see the fire was still lit. It was.

'I went out with her, because I didn't know – I didn't know what to do, because all the other lads had a girl ...'

'So you …'

'I asked her in the first place because I had to take somebody to the debs. Everyone was taking some girl or other. I couldn't go alone. And it would've been odd to bring one of my sisters with me. They wouldn't have gone anyway. And I couldn't stay at home because I would have been the only one in my class not there. What else could I do?' I said, amazed I had managed to get that much out.

'How do I know what you should have done? Couldn't you just be like everyone else … that, that or stay home?' There was something about the way he said 'home'.

'I couldn't,' I said, 'not forever. It's not that I didn't try …' I thought it best to go no further, afraid he wouldn't understand.

'So that's what brings you up to Dublin so much,' he said, glad to have worked that much out for himself.

'Yes. Yes, I suppose,' I answered. What else could I say?

'And we were all convinced you had a woman up there. People asking me if we'd met her yet … or when we'd get to see her. Auntie Nora asking just the other day when we'd have the next wedding … thinking a year after your mother's death would be okay.'

'Auntie Nora doesn't have to worry about me. She never got married herself anyway did she,' I said, blushing right away at the implication I was making.

'Up to Dublin! Huh.' He spoke to himself. 'Dublin's quare and dangerous,' he added, in a way that didn't require an answer.

He turned around, his back to the range, and shuffled over to the kitchen table. Then he tilted the milk-cooler with his two hands to pour some milk into the jug until it was nearly overflowing. Ready to get a damp cloth and clean it up if I had to, I was glad when he didn't spill so much as a drop. I felt awkward and ashamed sitting there watching him do this – my job, usually. He poured the milk that wouldn't go in the jug into the saucepan for the calves, and set it on the side of the range to heat it up until the cows were milked. After that, he would see to the calves themselves. He lifted the enamel milk-bucket that was always set on the table-rails once it was cleaned every morning after milking. Next, he gave it a good scalding with hot water from the kettle – water boiled so long that it had the kettle singing earlier. He set the kettle, with its mouth turned in, back down on the side of the range so that it wouldn't boil over with the heat. Then he swirled the scalding water around the bottom of the bucket and emptied it in one go into the calves' saucepan. He stretched over a bit to grab the dish-cloth off the rack above the range, then he dried the bucket and hung it up again rather carelessly, watching to see it didn't roll down on top of the range. It didn't.

All at once, he straightened up as if a thought had suddenly struck him. He turned round and looked at me for a second, our eyes meeting and taking each other in. The look he gave now was different from the earlier one – the sudden teary glance he gave me when I had first told him. Now I noticed the wrinkles across his forehead, some curled, some squared off, the short grey hair pulled down in a fringe, the eyebrows, the eyes. What eyes! They chased away whatever daydream was going through my mind just then. They made me want to run. Those eyes that could say so much without a word. I knew then that the only way to look at a man was right in the eyes, even if it was a casual side-glance, on the sly … I looked away, unable to take any more, grateful that he took it upon himself to speak. He had the bucket tucked up under his arm the way he did when he was going out milking.

'And what about your health?' he managed to say, nervously. 'Is your health all right?'

'Oh, I'm fine. Fine,' I replied quick as I could, more than glad to be able to give such a clear answer. I started tapping my fingers. Then it struck me just what he was asking.

'God preserve us from the like of that,' he said over his shoulder to me, facing the door. You could tell he was relieved.

'You don't have to worry,' I said, trying to build his trust, having got that far. 'I'm careful. Very careful. Always.'

'Can you be a hundred percent careful?' he added curiously, his voice more normal. 'I mean, if half what's in the Sunday papers and the week's television is true.'

I let him talk away, realising he probably knew much more than I thought. Wasn't the television always turned towards him, with all sorts of talk going on in some of the programmes while he sat there in the big chair with his eyes closed, dozing by the fire, it seemed, but probably taking it all in.

He took his coat down off the back of the door, set it over the chair.

'And did you have to tell me this secret of yours – at my age?'

'Yes, and no.' I had said it before I realised, but I continued: 'Well, I'm not saying I had to, but I was afraid you'd hear it from someone else, afraid someone would say something about me with you there.' I thought I was getting through. 'I thought you should know anyway. I thought you were ready.'

'Ready! I'm ready now all right. And are you telling me people round here know?' he said sourly.

'Yes, as it happens. You can't hide anything. Especially in a remote place like this.'

'And you think you can stay around here?' he exclaimed in what sounded to me like horror. His words hit me so quickly I didn't know whether they were meant as a statement or a question. Did they require an answer? From me – or from him? I wondered. Sure, I was intending or rather, I should say, happy to stay. He was my father. And I was the youngest, the only son. My two sisters were married and living in London. So it was down to me. Even though my sisters had convinced me the night before they went back that there was always a place for me in London if I needed it.

Surely, he should have known I would want to stay. Who else would look out for him? Help with the few animals we had, look after the house, keep an eye on our tiny bit of a farm, see he was all right, take him to mass on Sunday, and keep him company? '*And you think you can stay around here ...*' I repeated, none the wiser, still trying to work out whether I was to take it as a question or a statement, and if he expected an answer or not.

He had dragged his Wellingtons over between the chair and the head of the table, and was bent down struggling to undo the laces of his hobnailed boots. He looked different that way. If I had to go ... I said to myself. If he threw me out and told me he didn't want to see or have anything more to do with me ...

I remembered at once some of my friends and

acquaintances in Dublin. The ones who were kicked out by their families when they found out. Mark, whose father called him a dirty bastard and told him not to come near the house again as long as he lived. Keith, whose dad gave him a bad beating when he discovered he had a lover, and who kept him locked up at home for a month even though he was nearly twenty. Philip, who was under so much stress he had a nervous breakdown, who had no option but to leave his teaching job after one of his worst pupils saw him leaving a certain Sunday-night venue and the news spread by lunch-time the following Monday. The boys called him disgusting names right to his face, never mind the unconcealed whispers behind his back. Who could blame him for leaving, even if it meant the dole and finding a new flat across town? The dole didn't even come into it for Robin. His parents gave him twenty-four hours to clear out of the house and take all he had with him, telling him he wasn't their son anymore, that he had brought all this on himself, and that they never wanted to see him again as long as he lived. Which they didn't. They came home that night to find his body laid out on the bed in their room, empty pillboxes on his chest, half a glass of water under the mirror on the dressing table, a short crumpled note telling them that his only wish was to die where he was born, that he loved them and was sorry he hurt them but saw no other way.

The slow-rolling chimes of the clock interrupted my litany. He was still opposite me, struggling hard to get into his wellies, his trouser legs tucked down inside his thermal socks. If I had to go, I thought to myself, I would never see my father like this again. Never. The next time I would see him, he would be stone-cold dead in his coffin, his three children returning home together on the first plane from London after an urgent phone call telling us he was found slumped in the garden, or that they weren't sure if he fell in the fire or was dead before the fire burnt the house to the ground overnight, or maybe they would find him half-dressed in the bedroom after some of the neighbours had broken down the door ... as they tried to work out when they had last seen him alive, no one able to work out the exact time of death.

He had got the better of his Wellingtons now and had straightened himself up. Wrapped in his greatcoat, with his cap in one hand, about to put it on, he stood there, for a moment, indecisively, with the enamel milk-bucket wedged under his arm.

Then he moved slowly, tottered almost, over to the front door. My eyes followed his face, his side, his back, his awkward steps away from me while his last words of a moment ago kept going round and round in my head like an eel scooped out of a well on a hot summer day and set on a big flagstone.

He paused at the door the way he always did on his way out and dunked his finger in the holy-water font hung up on the door-jamb. It was an old wooden font with the Sacred Heart on it that my mother brought back from a pilgrimage to Knock the time the Pope was over. I could see him trying to bless himself, not even sure if it was the finger or thumb he had dipped in the holy water he was using.

He placed his hand on the latch, opened the door and pulled it towards him.

Then he turned round, headfirst, his body following slowly, and looked at me. His stare was so direct that my mind stopped racing and my thoughts recoiled at once to their dark corners.

'Will you stand by the braddy cow for me while I'm milking her?' he asked. 'She still has that sore teat.'

Translated by Frank Sewell with Úna Ní Chonchúir

SEVEN HUNDRED WATCHES

Somewhere in this city is a shop – if you could call it that – and it only opens one day in the year. Naturally enough this day never falls on the same date, since each year is a muddle of three hundred and sixty-five days. Of course as to this particular shop, very few are in the know and the cognoscenti keep it to themselves. They really don't give a hoot about it and care little who does, as long as they are not reminded of it. They steer clear of it. They know what they are about, or like to believe so. They're indifferent. Maybe you are too, if you're anything like them.

I am far from indifferent. I went in there once, on an impulse, propelled by my own two feet on a chance visit to the city. That's why I'm no longer indifferent, and if you find yourself there some day, you too will no longer be indifferent. I'm still there, you see. I'm here, waiting for you ...

I was on a visit to the city, a walkabout. One of those mindless days with nothing grabbing my attention, not a living thing. You know the way it is. Loafing about, unsure about the universe, down one street, up another and sometimes halfway down a street I had walked five minutes previously before the onset of vague déjà vu. You could say I was in a trance-like state with a hint of ennui. You can be sure that it's easier to find yourself in the metropolitan maze than to get out of it, as a rustic philosopher remarked in days gone by. And I continued my saunterings. Now and again I would stop and stare at a window, checking a price before deciding it was beyond my reach, examine an item of furniture that I did not require, give ear to distant muzak pouring from a premises. Such were my vacant ways on that shambolic day. My mind was free or perhaps astray, half-dreaming, half-conjuring up things and, fleetingly, in a state of no-mind.

And yet I was happy for reasons unknown to me. The world was my oyster until I wended my way down a cul-de-sac, at the end of which stood a shop with a small yellow door. At first I failed to distinguish its name and, looking closely, discovered it had none, something that excited my curiosity. Nothing at all in that murky window, but an old-fashioned clock that had stopped long ago, a clock you'd never find today except in a disused convent or an antique store. Yes, I said to myself, there might be something here and, as I had a few hours of the afternoon to idle away, in I went. The door creaked as I entered. I've never liked proclaiming my entrance or attracting the attention of shopkeeper or assistant – especially if I had no intention of buying anything.

Snakes alive! Not a sinner in sight. The hovel contained hundreds of watches, crouched on shelves and counters and, when space had run out, dangling from the ceiling. Hundreds, maybe thousands of watches ... They were a mystery to behold and those that still functioned played their part as though in an orchestra of crickets – little twelve-eyed insects in a most unnerving harmony. Each had its own dignity and I noticed how jealously they preserved their own space, their luminous integrity. I was watching, each and every one, from row to row, from shelf to shelf, up down, down up.

The world was a pulsing watch. The previous world had stopped. I took courage, grabbed a watch and examined it.

'It's yourself!' I startled. I turned around to see whose voice it was ...

He was leaning over the counter, hands propping his face. From my vantage point he appeared to be a hunchback, but he might have been different had he stood erect. He was a wizened, triangular-skulled creation; a blue-rinsed mop that was in need of a hay-fork, protruding black eyebrows like some remote bramble bush and the wrinkled face on him could only be likened to the skin of an anorexic elephant's ears. My immediate impulse was to laugh and to ask him did his hair know what a comb was. I didn't, of course. He was not a pleasing sight, but I didn't inform him of this. Would you?

'Just browsing,' I said, picking up another watch with feigned interest. His face was a thousand times more interesting that that of the watch. When next I raised my head he had his back turned to me – rather rudely I thought – and appeared to be winding a watch. I picked up another watch, and yet another. I noted their shape, colour, make, weight and sound. I was amazed at how little interest he had in me, fumbling and toying with his watches behind the counter. I spied him out of the corner of my eye. When he had wound one of them he would lay it aside, look around, pause and pick up another, and yet another and another again. He continued for quite some time. I was sure he would call me and persuade me to buy one, but strange as it may seem, I might not have been there at all as far as he was concerned as he pottered around picking up watches that needed winding. This pleased me no end as I have a distaste for those callous salesmen who would persuade a corpse to buy life insurance. He might have been a grotesque figure, but at least he left me alone to browse among the watches …

Time flew as I looked at them, admiring their variety. Something, I felt, was needling me … Do you know not one of them had a price-tag and, more remarkable still, no pair told the same time. This only fuelled my curiosity. I looked again, here and there, but sure enough not one synchronised with the other. I wonder, I reflected, are they all in competition, in a race, or jealously guarding their own time and space, independent of each other? Or are they all part of a team that ensures that every living second is covered? If that is the case they're having me on and everybody else to boot, except it appears that anyone with a grain of sense steers clear of this place. But why, I asked myself, if they are able to keep time, as dutiful watches, why have they all gone wonky, if they are wonky? Or is it me? It is often difficult to distinguish between the normal person and one with a question mark over him. Practically the same …

But speaking of time, what hour of the day is it, I asked myself and looked at my watch. Quarter to two. Quarter to shit! It must have stopped. I put my wrist to my ear. Dead as a dodo. I shook my hand. Again. The bastard had stopped to be sure. Now what would I do not being able to tell the time, surrounded by a flock of watches and not one of them you could trust, judging by their antics. If I approached Quasimodo, he'd try to sell me a watch for sure, and who could blame him? Already he was squinting at me as though he sensed I had a dilemma.

'You are bereft of time,' he muttered, putting a watch aside and taking up another. I agreed. What else could I do?

'Had you looked after it well,' said he, 'it wouldn't have let you down.'

'What looking after? All a watch needs is winding. It's not an infant that needs its botty oiled twice a day!'

'Ah, were it as simple as that,' he sighed, shaking his head heavily and looking at another watch. 'I speak, you see, not of the watch, but of time.'

No, I'm not going to argue with him, I told myself. He seemed the debating type and that was the last thing on my mind. I'd think of an excuse to be off.

'What time is it anyway?' I asked politely.

'What time do you require?'

'What do you mean what – ?' my hackles beginning to rise. 'What is the fucking time?'

'Right now?'

'Yes, yes, this instant!' There was tension in my voice.

'But that depends on the time you require.'

'I do not require ...'

'But didn't you ask ...?'

'I merely asked you for the time because I need to know.'

'And what need have you any more of time?'

'Is that any concern of yours?'

'Whether it is or not, I do not give of my time, gratis, to all and sundry, not knowing beforehand what need they have of it.'

'Your time?'

'My time, yes. Isn't that what you want?'

'The time is yours now, I suppose.'

'If it's not, why are you asking me?'

'Now look here, sir!' I was agitated by now and I'm sure it was clear from my voice. 'I simply require the time. If you are not prepared to give it, fine – but just say so. If you are prepared, give it to me now and cut the shite, okay?'

'But how can I give you something which you already have ...?'

'I don't have the fucking time and ...'

'Not knowing the reason you require it, since you refuse to tell me.'

'Okay, why do I require it, why do I require the time? ... because my wife has an appointment with the dentist at three o'clock.'

'Your poor wife has an appointment with the dentist at three o'clock?'

'Yes, to extract a rotten tooth, if you must know, and I must get home and drive her to the dentist.'

'And are you one hundred percent sure that the rotten tooth is not yours?'

I grabbed an old clock from the table beside me and decided if I got hold of him I wouldn't leave a tooth, rotten or sound, in his head.

'Waste of time trying to knock a tooth out of me with that clock,' he remarked, 'since all I've got is plastic teeth and not one of them rotten, as false teeth do not decay. Anyway I keep them clean, but I'll tell you the time if you have an appointment ...'

'My wife, I told you, at three o'clock.' I put the clock aside and retreated a step or two.

He looked around, paused, and looked around again. Then he stretched out his hand and picked up a watch in front of him.

'Well then, it's three o'clock,' he said, nonchalantly, peeking over his spectacle frames.

'What's this *well then*? That watch isn't right.'

'Every single watch here is in order,' he stated, somewhat sternly. 'It's you that's out of order. Every watch here has the right time. Don't insult my watches!'

'The right time, eh?'

'Be sure of it, with the exception of that nonsensical trinket on your wrist which has no time at all – except time that has ceased – and that isn't time at all.'

I was becoming stressed out again. No, not stress, frenzy, feverish frenzy. And yet, somehow, I managed to restrain myself.

'And let us say,' said I, attempting to put this ridiculous ball into his own court, 'let us say my wife's appointment was for four.'

'With the dentist ... the rotten tooth.'

'Never mind the tooth ... if the appointment was for four, it would be four o'clock now according to your way of looking at things.'

'The way the world looks at things, not me. But you're perfectly correct,' he said. 'I'm glad you're getting a glimmer of things at last.'

I didn't answer him. What was the point? No sense arguing with this fellow at all. For the sake of peace I'd buy a watch – that might shut him up – and hightail it out of this joint.

He had gone back to his watches. In a fit I took off my own watch. I gave it a good rattle, but if a million earthquakes erupted under its navel it wouldn't come to life. I looked around once more at the watches until I picked one that looked user-friendly enough. I'd buy it if it were at all reasonable. He would put the right time on it, hopefully, and I would make my escape.

'Excuse me,' I said, to attract his attention.

'Oh, you're still there,' he said, feigning surprise. 'Thought I heard you slipping out a while ago.'

'I'll buy a watch,' I said, handing it to him, 'if the price is right.'

'No can do,' he said with a churlish shake of the head. 'None of the watches here is priced.'

'What?'

'Not one; do you not get it yet? Time isn't for sale. When are people going to stop buying and selling? They'll never learn.' He shook his head gravely. Sorrow had invaded his face.

'You're saying that the watches here are not for sale?'
'Oh, none of these watches will ever be sold. You don't think you're in some terrestrial shop, do you?'

I didn't know what to do. I looked into his two eyes, trying to figure out what kind of a gobshite he might be. If I had taken a few pints I'd have smashed his face in before he knew what time it was. It was difficult to know whether to sympathise or to be angry with him, but it was becoming plain that there was little point in locking horns with him.

'If it's not a shop, what is it?' I asked with as much civility as I could muster.

'Don't you realise,' says he, pretending to be astonished, 'that it's merely a waiting room for watches, watches like you and the world.'

'Like me? Waiting for what?' I asked, while telling myself

I might as well humour him if we were going to get to the bottom of this.

'Oh, that I can't say,' he retorted, 'such a ponderous question you should ask yourself, or the watches, but it's unlikely that they would satisfy you with an answer. The whole world's waiting and we haven't a clue what we're all waiting for ...'

'I see,' I said. It was balderdash, of course. 'And you can't sell me any of these watches?'

'It's not right to sell,' he said sombrely, and sorrow had once more invaded his being. 'Selling is not right and people are breaking the law ten days a week. I'm sure you've seen them. Advertisements everywhere. Selling, selling, selling and earmarking everyone! Some of them sell the same things twice and even three times. Others sell stolen property, or stuff that isn't theirs to sell, and more of them sell themselves – soul and body.' He drew a breath. 'Nothing to do with me, as long as you're not one of them ... But there's one good thing you can sell,' says he, and I could see he was chuffed by the attention I was paying to his rant; 'your watch is kaput, but you can sell it to me and I'll only ask you for twenty euros.'

I was nonplussed. I drew a breath. It took me a while to figure out his offer. I felt like the bird in the cuckoo clock with a dose of laryngitis.

'I can ... I can sell my own watch ... to ... to you,' I stammered, 'and throw in twenty quid while I'm at it? That would leave me minus my banjaxed watch and minus twenty euros. What sort of a deal is that? That's robbery, mate, daylight robbery!'

'It mightn't sound like a good deal to someone who's a bit astray, but it's the right deal for you at this point in your life. Right now, this minute! And I'll set your watch going again. Isn't that what you want?'

Like a big eejit – and to this hour I don't know what prompted me – I took out my last twenty euro note and handed it to him, with the watch. And do you know what? I was rather pleased with the transaction.

He took the watch without looking at it. Instead he looked at all the other watches in his den – those on shelves and tables, those dangling from the ceiling and his beady eye roamed from one to the other.

'Got it,' he said finally with a wink, his mouth breaking into a smile, a twinkle forming in his eye. 'I've discovered a time previously unknown, a time that no other watch has. How fortunate you are!' The smile had crept fully across his face. He fixed the time on the watch-face and opened up the back. Taking a little plastic bag from his jacket pocket he picked out what appeared to be a tiny white tablet. This he crushed into powder between his thumbnails and deposited the dust into the watch's womb.

'Now,' says he, 'that'll keep you going for a good while, maybe forever.' He closed the back of the watch and shook it close to his ear, as though concocting a cocktail.

A fog descended on my brain. The two of us looked at the watch. The hands were at it like blazes, scything away for all their worth. My heart rose.

'Now,' says he, 'do you see that! Do you hear it? The purring of a kitten that's got the cream.'

'What was that white stuff you put into it?'

'Do you not know? What galaxy are you from at all?

That's crack, lad, the hottest dope around. Mighty big in America, as they say, and it's cheap too.'

'And you're peddling dope to these wretched watches?' I said, looking all around me, my eyes beginning to water almost.

'That's all they want, lad. It's the dope that keeps them ticking over – sure isn't it keeping the whole world going? Sure yeah, all these watches are doped to the gills, high as kites ... some are stoned on cannabis, others on coke, more on grass, a lot on E, LSD, speed, ice – the lot. Crack's the latest.'

'They like the crack?'

'Mad for it. Wired to the moon half of the time, hyperactive, schizophrenic, zonked, but full of devilry and the joys of life. Can't you see yourself all twelve eyes of them popping out of their heads and the way their hands are going, the fast lane, eh? None of them at the same speed, none having the same time, and that's the way they like it, and that's the way the world should be. Boring old farts they're not, or feckless fools going around imitating each other – but they have a certain rustic pigheadedness and humanity about them, and if they're not having a good time I don't know who is.'

'And you're the one who keeps them going?'

'Myself and God's spirit. Oh, it's hard work I'm telling you. My perspiration alone would fill buckets.' He picked up another watch. 'Winding and winding. We do our best. What else can anyone do? A lot depends on us. Trying to get the time, keeping the time going, putting in time, stopping time, seizing the hour from time to time whenever possible. Time and tide wait for no man, time belongs to no one and we only have it on loan, to keep going as long as we can, as long as we can ...'

'And it's here that time and all the time in the world is kept going?'

'It's all here. All time resides here – and simple folk think there's nothing going on here. They haven't the time to come in even. They haven't time to do this or time to do that. Nobody has time anymore for God or man or beast, not to mention time for time. The poor ignorant savages. They avoid this place, poor things. If only they knew that all time is encapsulated here. Anyone who finds himself here hasn't the time or the inclination to leave. And there's loads of time here for anyone who wants to come looking for it – if they only knew. They wouldn't have to do anything else again for the rest of their lives, simply pause for a second outside the door and slink in, like you.'

'Like me?'

'Oh, yes, lad, just like you.'

Translated by Gabriel Rosenstock

THE BOOK OF SIN

The monsignor was a liar. His curate was almost as bad. Most people would choke on their own lies eventually, but not these two. With them, one lie propped up another like planks of wood in a cross-beam. It was hard for her to tell who spoke first, their voices rising and dipping like a row of oars scooting through the sea. But it didn't matter. It was always the same old hobby horse's shite they kept going on about anyway. Half of it not even true. Including what they were saying about death. She was sure of that, the old woman. She knew they were lying to her from day one. What would they know about death anyway? No more than teenagers getting curious and messing around with Ouija boards or whatever. But teenagers were more honest. They didn't try to drag everybody into what they were up to, but kept out of the way, clueless. They certainly didn't let on that they knew what it was all about like some monsignor and priest, or priest and monsignor, laying down the law to her about life and death as if they had the inside track. What would they know more than anybody else who hadn't died and come back yet? The way she saw it, no one alive could speak about death because it had nothing to do with this world one way or the other. Death belonged solely to the next world. In fact, death *was* the next world. It didn't have a halfpence worth of interest in this place. No one here would even recognise it if they saw it walk out in front of them. No one. And death didn't want to get mixed up in this world either, never mind come in and join it. Death was comfortable enough in its own place.

A bit like the old woman herself, half-content with her lot, even though she could no longer move. From the way she was lying on the bed, you would think, at first glance, that she had just tumbled into it by accident, rather than that she had been lying there these past two years since her bad fall on the stairs. At least she was free from pain – apart, that is, from the buzzing irritation, the droning sermonising in her ear from the monsignor and his curate. And her lying there, drained of life, not fully conscious most of the time. One minute there, two minutes not. Thank God for those moments out of it. Drifting away forever. For good. Any day, any moment now. Her two feet on the brink of the grave.

'It'll be easier to get to her now,' said the monsignor. 'I reckon she could go any time, pop her clogs, snuff it.'

'... Pop her clogs,' echoed the curate.

'Any time now. Any minute ... she could kick the bucket.'

'... Kick the bucket.'

'Did you bring the paper?'

'... Paper.'

'The tabloid.'

'... Tabloid.'

'Aye, the wee red-top. Give it to me. It'll pass the morning, and some of the afternoon too, if need be. You know, this one might drag it out late tonight or tomorrow even.'

'... Tomorrow ...'

Tomorrow. The word started an itch in her ear that she couldn't scratch. Stung her like a winged insect that she couldn't shoo away, or like a creepy-crawly that she just couldn't block from going deeper and deeper into her ear. Tomorrow, she thought drowsily. There was really no such day. There never was. Them ones going on about tomorrow as if they knew anything about it. They should know better: there is no tomorrow in this life. It's not going to come in through the door and warm its arse in front of the fire any time today now, is it?

Yesterday they could talk about all they liked. There would be some sense in that. Everyone alive has some handle on yesterday, and some chance of understanding it. But tomorrow? Well, there they were, the great educated monsignor, him and his curate getting it all wrong about something as plain and simple as that! Or were they just trying to deceive people?

'In some states in America, men are allowed to marry each other,' said the monsignor, his eyes widening at the newspaper he was holding.

'... Men marry each other!' rhymed the curate, barely able to look over his shoulder at the paper.

'Women in Maryland can receive up to twenty thousand dollars if they rent out their bodies for nine months to have children for rich strangers. That's nearly fifteen thousand euros, isn't it?'

'... Fifteen thousand euros. Some of the stories are hard to believe ...'

'A tornado flattened eight thousand houses in Texas and left thirty thousand homeless. Hope it doesn't hit Ireland.'

'... Tornado in Ireland. That tornado story isn't very interesting, is it? Too disturbing. Too upsetting. Are there no juicier tales?'

'Hold on,' said the monsignor, turning a page. 'What about this! A TD who picks up prostitutes three nights a week and drives them back to his hotel.'

'… Three nights, now … women or boys?'

'Wait, wait till I see. Oh, and all the kinky things they get up to in the hotel.' The monsignor's eyes were widening.

'… Kinky things … how kinky?'

'Ah, you know, belts and handcuffs and what-have-you.'

'… Belts and handcuffs.'

'They give him a service that they call here "a good old spanking".'

'… Spanking.'

'And they wear nylon stockings, apparently.'

'Oh … those kind of women … I wonder …'

'And this TD gets so much on expenses that he can pay for the whores out of his allowance.'

'… His allowance. Isn't God good to him,' said the curate. 'If I wasn't a priest, I'd be a politician.'

Who was it who said they were all the same – politicians and churchmen? The churchmen with their bright angelic robes. But they weren't all the same to the old woman. She could tell good from bad. Or so she thought. But she didn't like most of them. The way they tried to bamboozle people. And they succeeded, too, unfortunately. Coming across all soft and sweet. Kind and caring. Friendly – to your face. And each of them lurking in the other's shadow …

'This woman here,' said the monsignor. 'Open the Book of Sin to see the whoppers she got up to in her day. See if she can be forgiven at all. See what sort of purgatory she's in for, if it's not a red hot roasting in hell.'

'… Purgatory …'

Purgatory. They ought to be ashamed talking about purgatory. Hadn't she spent her whole life in purgatory ever since they boxed her into it when she was still in her prime. Soon, they would probably be saying that there was no purgatory. That there had been some change. Again. Sure hadn't they shut down limbo after it was all the rage when she was young! Now there was no limbo at all – not even for anyone stupid enough to believe their lies. So what about all the poor unbaptised children who had gone – or were supposed to have gone – to limbo? Where were they hidden away now if there never was a limbo? Somebody somewhere had made a terrible mistake; but he wasn't the one to be pitied. Not him, but the poor broken-hearted mothers who were taken in by their dogma. Like the woman she knew who had nine stillborn children – nine in nine years. All gone to limbo, the church authorities said, one after the other. They would feel no pain, the holy fathers said, but would never get to see their maker. It was God's will, they said. That was just the way of it, and the children could never, ever, ever leave, they said, even though they had done no wrong. Tainted with original sin, they would never see the light, the face, of God, they said. They wouldn't be floating merrily at the Gates of Heaven ready to greet the mother who bore them in pain. And the mother believed it all. She and generations like her. Every word of it. For it was the priest who had said it, wasn't it? Said it, right from the altar.

And now they had thrown limbo out the window. Some Johnny-come-lately did away with it in a flash, like as not. With one civil, servile stroke of his pen. Where was the same Johnny-come-lately for all those generations when fathers had to bury the tear-washed corpses of their children at night in boundary ditches? The youngsters these days were right. The young who paid no heed whatsoever to the clergy, sacraments or mass. The young spending Sunday mornings sitting on drystone walls near the chapel gates, talking out loud in their own lingo about sport and fashion … The clergy with their limbo and their purgatory – hell, slap it into them!

Next thing – if she lived long enough to see it – they would probably be saying there was no hell. That it – if anyone was still listening to them – did not exist either. Sure, weren't they already saying there was no fire – that hell was 'a state' – when they used to let on it was one gigantic blaze with devils gathered all around and poking sinners with pointy red pikes … But hell, for sure, was here on earth. Hadn't they damned her to there often enough during her own lifetime? Purgatory and hell were of this world, not the next. And if she didn't hurry up and die, maybe even heaven would shut up shop before she got there.

'What sort of butterfingers have you? Is that Book of Sin not open yet?'

'Give us a chance,' said the curate, hurriedly flicking through the much-thumbed book. 'What section do you want?'

'God's Commandments, of course. Anyone, even a saint, could be caught out there, you know. That's where the tally is kept to make up the final reckoning.'

'… Final reckoning … Wait a sec, monsignor. I have them.'

'Number Six. Six. That's the juicy one. Go straight to Number Six.'

'Six. Six.'

'Number Six. Thou shalt not lust.'

'Lust. Lust it is. L – U – S for LUST …'

'Aye, the rest don't really matter, you see. We don't even have to check them. But Number Six is the biggie. Oh, many's the man or woman comes out tops in the other nine, but, damn it, Number Six turns out tricky for them; so slimy and slippery that even a holy bishop could tumble and get into trouble, if he wasn't careful …'

'I have it. I have it now.'

'And what symbol is it?'

'A big red spot.'

'And so it would be. It would. A big red spot. I can nearly see it from here, blind and all as I am. I could have guessed it. Ah, I always get it right under pressure from the job. I don't even have to check half the other commandments, but just head straight for that one. Number Six, every time.'

'And what does the big red spot mean?'

'That she fell, you pleb. She fell. Sin of the flesh, of course. A great big red-hot sin of the flesh …'

Flesh. Flesh. But there was flesh and there was flesh. The clergy led people up the garden path about that one, too. Don't eat flesh on a Friday, they said. Thou shalt not! They didn't anyway, the poor creatures. So many with empty, rumbling stomachs. Their gnarled guts growling together in a chorus … Fast and abstinence, they said. And no call for it at all. Good Friday. It was a Good Friday her pregnant sister fell weak from hunger and cracked her skull on the floor. They said that was the will of God, too. She had hidden a joint of meat in a dish in the kitchen cupboard away from flies and midges. Smelt out three days later, it was fed to the dogs. She left behind seven children. Seven children – all under eight years old. They could have done with the meat then – with no one to fend for them. No one but her … Them and their flesh. They were fattening themselves up with it now though – seven days a week. Seven days a week, Friday and all. The monsignor and his curate tucking in to their beef or chicken. Afternoon *and* evening. Having their cake and eating it.

'And look at her now. The fallen woman. Her senses aren't much good to her now by the look of her.'

'… Not much good.'

'The woman who bore an illegitimate child.'

'… Illegitimate?'

'Yes. Illegitimate. I like that word, although there are some doing their level best to take the sting out of it, to devalue it, and banish it from people's mouths altogether or – even worse – make it a *good* word.'

'… A good word.'

'Ah, but if she could be purged of this sin! If she would only repent.'

'… Repent …'

'Go you round the other side of the bed and speak into her ear after me. I'll cover the ear on this side – in case she runs out of breath and gets no chance to repent at all.'

Her ears were already burning. Her life engine mocking her by keeping her going for the likes of these two to single her out and attack her *ex cathedra*. And the same two buckos no better than she was. The monsignor and his companion. The whelp afraid to say anything without the other's permission. Afraid to even think for himself. He'll be trained yet. The way hunters are. Him running after his master, then on ahead, attending to him like a sheepdog. Rounding up any doubting Thomas in the trembling herd.

Driving them on. Now, they were going to deafen her ears with one more blast right up to her last breath. You would think they were enjoying it.

And, oh, the terrible disappointment each time her consciousness returned, and her hearing and memory came back to her from some dark cave or other, her freedom giving way against her will. The heavy disappointment at still being in this world, a prisoner of consciousness, knowing she was here ... still here. She had never understood death properly until, several times, she felt herself drifting outside of her earthly body. It was good to drift outside life. Good to die and not be sucked in by life, or for her to be sucking in a misguided world gone wrong. It was good, this drift deathwards, even if it wasn't full death, but some temporary hitch of a death, an interregnum ... until real definite death finally showed up.

'O my God, I am heartily sorry for having offended thee.'

'And I detest my sins above every other evil ...'

'Now and forever ...'

'Now and forever ...'

Angry. Angry. Always angry. Their voices rising up and beating into her inner ears. Like the noise she remembered of the ghetto blaster from the flat nextdoor when she lived in the city. She couldn't stick their yammering a moment longer. Day in, day out. Week after week, she'd had it for years, a lifetime. Her one and only lifetime. She was ready to explode. Really explode if she didn't get to speak one more time. Even now with life draining out of her, tiny movements appeared on her face, on her eyelashes and lips.

'The last wind! The last wind!'

'... Last wind.'

'Thanks be to God.'

'... To God ...'

'Now do you see the power of prayer? The good that comes from faith and praying?'

'... Praying ...'

'She's definitely trying to make her repentance. To return. The last confession.'

'... Repentance and last confession.'

'Before she passes ... before death claims her.'

'... Death, death.'

'Stop, stop. She's trying to talk. About her sin. To prepare herself for death.'

'... Prepare for death.'

'And you are wrong about death, too,' she said, suddenly. 'You're just trying to scare me. That's the way it is with you: bullying. Two big, lying, threatening bullies. Wrong about death, just as you are wrong about everything else. Life. Limbo. The flesh. And you're wrong about tomorrow, too. About sin, purgatory, hell ... about ... about everything under the sun. You can be nice sometimes ... very nice, but wrong all the same. You are just one big terrible mistake altogether. A thorn in the side of life, a rod on the back of the poor. All you do is mislead or confuse people about life, and you think you can play the same tricks on the dying. But I'll be safe, locked in the arms of death, with nothing to do but let it shelter and guide me to the end of time. And you, it's your job to scare us about it. But people don't need to be half as ready for death as you let on. That's no reason for living – spending all of our lives preparing to die ... Oh, no. This world doesn't understand death at all. And you don't understand it either. So don't try to tell me that you do, you pair of scheming liars, sour-faced gits, good-for-nothings ...'

The monsignor opened his mouth.

The curate opened his mouth.

'... How could you even begin to understand when death can't even get its nose past the door of this world. Not even its shadow as it flies past is countenanced here. Far from it. But death will have its day, with the help of God, its stinging victory, when this whole rotten world finally comes to an end.'

She stopped.

The curate's mouth fell shut.

Translated by Frank Sewell

THE ROCK

It had always been there, you could say. One ginormous rock. Vast and powerful in size. Just a quarter of it would weigh hundreds of tons on any scale. It wasn't a rock, but the mother of all rocks. A giant of a rock. A god among rocks. Sitting there at ease, on the top of the hill, as cosily as if it had been tipped lovingly into place by the hand of God. It ruled. And no one else. A powerful, commanding ruler. Imperious looking, unknown to and despite itself. But there it was, interrupting thousands of glances at the mysterious, multicoloured hem of the sky. The rock giving way to no one's stare or side glance, no matter how keen, strong or imploring. Instead, it thanked them by eclipsing their view and turning them into submissive bent-necked slaves. Weighed down firmly, it stood its ground with daunting authority. Silent. Deadly silent. Wrapped in the ancient dreamy silence of the ages. Forever changing the look of its wrinkled, rocky body – with its hundreds of bony cheeked slopes, knee-like bends, calf-shaped curves, cocked-ear edges, swellings, brows, warts, pimples, lumps, eyes, hard skin, split ends, trillions of features.

You sensed from the whole angry looking precipice of its head that the rock had seen all things. And it didn't even have to try. It just saw, unconsciously, the whole countryside all around. Broad-backed fields. Small, green hillocks. Good open grassland. Stretches of barbed wire fence. Gaps. Cliffs. Strong ridges. Clefts and fissures. Bare slabs of rock. Long flat areas of stone, some coated in mildew. And gardens. An abundance of them. Shaped in squares, circles or triangles. Others irregular in shape. Rough-hewn paths. Soft damp bogs. Curving streams half-hidden from view. Deep glens stretching out way into the distance. And, lower down, wide harbours, narrow creeks, straits, man-made quays, bright wide beaches sometimes boxed in by the turning tide. The free, migrant ocean …

The rock was like the wise old grandmother of them all. A taciturn grandmother who didn't pay much heed to her charges but who was always there. Like a seasoned old-timer in a rocking chair, keeping her eye on them all. A guardian angel watching from a distance. Reserved, maybe even half-deaf. Looking like she was just dozing away.

That was its life. That was all its seized up backbone had ever known. Acres and acres of years wound up inside her. Hundreds of them. Thousands. Millions. All of them contained beneath its crust. The tough outer layers and hard edges that gladly let the lichen nest there, breeding, springing and germinating. Stretching out to grow into a fine healthy coating on its rough skin.

Now the rock was there so long, it hardly remembered its origins. All it had was a raked up memory of the wild upheaval that went into its making, long before the far-distant time of the earth's second phase. The only pain it had ever known was the great push towards birth. Its only growing pains, the primal-screaming explosion of creation long, long ago.

It was as though it had grown there, right where it was

born, set and settled down. Here, the rock was boss. Gradually, over generations, nature's greedy instincts and desires had been overcome. Their attacks had never worn it down.

The ice block. The ice block that had served for hundreds of years as a white, frozen sheet or shroud, melted at last. Melted slowly. Skirred downwards into millions of bashful, yielding drops, in a meandering stream carving their own path as they went. And frost. The black frost didn't get to stick its fangs in deep enough even to tickle the rock. The frost could always be laughed off easily if it went too far. The same with the sun – the sun with its sulky, deadly shafts of light stretching down on the rock's head, right into its eyes, like needles. The same poor sun couldn't split a stone, never mind a giant rock. So the sun's heat never really encroached. Never burnt through its skin or left a lasting mark any more than fire did. Fire. That rush of sparks that consumed all growth, plants, roots and scraws, but didn't even singe the surface layers of the rock. All it did was leave behind a smattering of black dust on the surface of its giant body – a shadow that was scrubbed away by the cleansing efforts of time and rain. Rain in its own shapeless form or in its hard-hitting suit of hail. The rain and the crafty snow: a quare dancing duo. They had sought to wear down the rock with their toe tapping. But the rock's surface had blunted, chipped and destroyed the hidden teeth of their high heels. They, too, were exhausted. Left dizzy many times by the insatiable, puffed-up air streaming past. Air. The dreamy, sweeping air packing itself into all kinds of pockets about the rock. The air was all lovey-dovey at first, gently combing the edges of the rock like the studious hand of a sculptor. Then it would get curious, stroking the rock's surface, whispering and whistling to it. Coming back again and again like a bad dream, then suddenly bursting out in a sapping thunderstorm, blasting the rock, keening, besieging and beseeching.

But the bare rock didn't give in. Didn't bend, bow, lie down, move aside or step back. No, it stood up, bold, daring and undaunted. An enormous tuft on the bare patch of hill, its hilltop dwelling. The rock paid none of them any heed. It stood stock-still and stubborn-as-you-like against them, holding its own individual shape, for all the biting cold that went into the hard clay where it stood. Cold was its staple diet but the rock didn't grow soft and ask or wish for anything else. Silent and still, it was just there, and would almost have gone unnoticed by the world, if it hadn't been for its bulk and breadth. And it had its own kind of peace there. Its own thoughts. Ancient wisdom. History. Its own soft dreamy silence made up of millions of years and stored in the marrow of its bones and in its heart. It was as if the rock had created its own spirituality, stored under its hunched back, just for itself, dating back to before man was ever dreamt of, never mind his fall....

Poor man. Two-legged, bow-legged. An earth-walker. The rock saw the soles of man track and spoil the carved-up crust of the whole world before and after him. Gradually coming closer towards the rock itself in halting and uneven steps. His shifting shape seemed strange and annoying; so out of place with all else in his surroundings, so odd and fidgety. Like a stray animal that hadn't learnt how to behave. Lacking solid and stable identity. A vague, curious guilt driving him on and on ... closer and closer to the rock. He probably didn't even know his way. And he would probably never reach the rock at all. Struggling under some burden, a heavy load that made him look as if he had a hump growing out of his back, weighing him down. At first the rock pitied him – twisted all out of shape like that. Unsure even of his own feet. Every gust of wind ready to blow him in one direction or the other. So easy to brush him away. Just a man. A human being. With not so much as a heel, foot or root in the ground.

Under the southwest face of the rock, the man stopped. By its side he was like a fly – a small, buzzing, irritating creature – but he laid hands on the rock as though it was his from time immemorial, every inch of it.

A diesel-powered drill bored a hole into its rear. Up, up into the rock's core. He shoved lighted sticks of gelignite, like shots of tranquiliser, into her. And ran like lightning away. Ran like a hare from hounds. The rock saw that much itself with its very own eyes. Saw it and –

The greedy air, always on the prowl, seized the cleared space for itself. Where the rock had been.

Translated by Frank Sewell

WITH THESE HANDS

To pull. To pull and score. Those were top of my wish list that Easter Saturday. I was dying for it. All het up for it. And I'd say there wasn't a mother's son in the whole club better turned out than me. I was a picture, even if I say so myself.

Queen of all I surveyed, I set myself up commandingly on a high stool. It'll show that I'm free and single, I thought. Open to offers. An official declaration of my availability for some brave soldier in the crowd. Me sitting there like a fancy item in a shop window during a sale. I could enhance the advertisement later with additional signs as necessary … if necessary. Because I really did look a picture, casually but carefully dressed in a black T-shirt with a glossy picture of Sinéad O'Connor on it, the height of fashion, ripped 501s so tight you'd think they were sprayed on, and white trainers. And I was clean-shaven, too, with plenty of Fahrenheit on me, my hair sitting well after this afternoon's wash, all slicked back with gel. Man, I was on for it, ready for the kill, as the bright young things here would say.

I hadn't been in such good form for ages, and it got better every time I lifted my pint to my lips or looked at the view from my high stool. There were loads of men in tonight, big men, slim men, and hunks too, by God, dancing and swaying before me: teenagers, men in their twenties, thirties, and some older. I looked them over one by one: up, down, across, back and front. My whole body was buzzing from top to toe, the blood in my veins swirling round and round like cream being churned to butter. I was horny, really horny, my conscienceless cock directing my gaze all over the place like a heedless compass suddenly gone mad and loving it. I wanted some soft round Easter eggs. Some sweet chocolate. Sweeter than sweet. Sure, I'd have to go on the hunt and make a catch before the end of the night. But I would and all. I believed in myself, in the spirit- and cock-raising night. It was a long time since I'd had so much faith in myself. You would have thought that I was high king of the whole kingdom pulsating in majesty all around me – with every father's son dancing for me at my royal prerogative – like it had all been carved from some magic dream by the hand of an artist.

I knocked back another drink. Looked around me again. Boy, this place was hot. Not warm now, but hot. Really hot. There was a 'ra-bounce' happening on the dancefloor. Music – if you could call it music. Dance – if you could call it dance. A rumpus and a ruckus. A real 'rooly-booly' as the nuns used to say at school yonks ago. Heads, arms and whole bodies swaying one way then the other on the crowded dancefloor, some spinning right round like they were dangling from the ceiling, caught in the rotating, multicoloured lights. Other guys wobbled like geese, or headed to mysterious dark spots in the room for a spark of inspiration. Boy, half the ones here were high and the other half getting there. And all the time, the temperature was rising and rising. Everyone pressed tight together. Packed in, body to body. Me, I was checking out the ones in front of me with my bedroom eyes. Sometimes all I could see were parts of them at a time: heads, shoulders, bellies, shapely behinds, their feet … whatever turned up in the flashing lights. I knew some of the lads here one way or another – to see, to touch. Some I knew well, others all too well. But thank God there were a fair few new ones here, too. It was them I was most interested in. My welcoming eyes kept being drawn to them like magnets. I liked the new, the fresh, the 'I'm not sure what type he is yet'. Oh, to suss out a new man! A new man with a new body, a new mind, a new everything, maybe … a stranger! To move in on a stranger. To touch him, enchant him, dominate him … someone who could put me under *his* spell, too. A special connection, maybe. One that could actually go somewhere. Be more than just a one-night stand. You never know.

And there he was! That is, if I could be sure in that crowd. With my roving eye on autopilot, I'd found him out. He was at the corner of the dancefloor the whole time, like he was hiding on me. A big strapping fella. Stocky, but not fat. With a light silky shirt and dark trousers. Short blonde hair and, as far as I could see, he was gorgeous. About thirty, or just under. No spring chicken, maybe, but he wasn't too old for me to have fun with. That's for sure. There was something different – fascinating – about him. Something very distinctive, but I couldn't say just what it was. The shirt, maybe. I was sure I'd never seen him in the club before. And I wanted him right away. There and then. Something about him really turned me on.

Who was he dancing with? I wondered. I'd have to find out. What if he had someone with him? It was hard to tell for sure. One minute he was looking one way, the next minute the other, or turning all the way around. Maybe he wasn't dancing with anyone in particular, but was on his own … God, let it be so.

I took another drink. Fixed my eyes upon him so they stuck to him, my hand under my chin, my legs crossed. I felt myself getting hard. He was the one. The one to go for. The way he kept swaying from side to side. All heart and legs, pumping and jumping to the beat. Sometimes he looked around him. You'd think our eyes would have met in silent acknowledgement, sooner or later. I was certainly close enough for him to see me, to notice me watching him, if he wanted to. All that was needed was for the lights to settle for a minute on me. Fat chance of that happening. Mostly, they were shining on his eyes and not me, although they could turn around any second if they were bumped into. Anyway, he was the one lit up by them the whole time – or so it seemed to me, anyway.

What's this? Did I see some fella getting interested and checking him out from behind? Dancing right next to him? Moving in on him? He fucking was, the bastard! He just went right up and rubbed his whole body against him. Familiar as you like! Rubbed his hand up and down his behind just like that. My man moved quickly to one side, glancing over his shoulder. He looked to see who it was. Then looked again, dismissively, to make sure. He drew back two or three steps. Well, a nod is as good as a wank to a wise man, so I took this as a warning. I'd have to be careful and get a move on. There were plenty of other hawkeyes on the lookout. If you didn't shake yourself and do something quick, fix your mark, you could end up leaving it too late. The worst thing would be to find out that he was free and easy all along, only to see him end up in the arms of somebody else. I took a bigger gulp, set down my glass and got up off my seat. Fast.

I made my way to the edge of the dancefloor. Shook my booty like a dog getting out of the water, just like the rest of them. I swayed and swung around, slyly winding my way through the moving bodies over towards the corner. In two minutes flat, I was opposite him, well aware in my heart of hearts that I'd hardly make a bolder, braver move all night than this one. He still hadn't noticed me, though. How could he have? But he would soon enough. I was not letting him get away. And what was the worst that could happen? A knock-back?

I danced in front of him – sometimes coming very close. He was bound to see me looking at him, watching him, checking him out. With his right hand, he wiped a layer of sweat from his head, running his fingers back through his short hair until his elbow nearly stuck into me. It looked like he knew I was watching him. I kept looking over: the two of us dancing away. Gradually, our body movements fell into the same swaying rhythm. Now my eyes lit up, ready to meet his, warmly, just as soon as he'd look at me, look into my eyes so full of love and welcome. One tiny second. That was all I needed. I waited and waited.

He'd take a drink all right, he said. He needed a break from dancing anyway. He was sweating. Water. That was all. He was driving, and you had to be careful in the city. I never liked paying a couple of euros for just a bottle of water when you could get something better for the same price. But each to his own, if that's what he wanted. Sure, the drinks were only an excuse anyway.

What was his name then? It didn't matter! Maybe it didn't matter, but still it would be nice to know. To know who I was talking to. It was only polite – trying to get to know each other like any two people. Maybe you're a Mickey or a Dickey, I said, or even a Willy?

He didn't answer, but he smiled all right. Then, after a pause, he said, Well, my name's John Paul, if you really want to know. Named after you-know-who, of course. I was born the day he came to Ireland, the poor sod. Now, then. You're talking to a man named after a pope, even if he's not so holy himself. He paused for a moment, bemused, and said: I'm Johnny. Tonight, you can call me Johnny.

He wouldn't have a smoke either. He didn't like fags. At least, not that kind! he confessed with another smile. He probably doesn't gamble either, I thought to myself. He's just what any mother would want: a son who doesn't drink, smoke, gamble, or womanise …

I asked where he was from, remembering I hadn't seen him before. The midlands. He obviously didn't want to be more specific. Okay! I wasn't going to hassle him. It didn't matter anyway. Up to the city for the weekend then, to get away for a bit? Not exactly. Just for tonight as he'd some work on tomorrow: a friend of his was away at a wedding and had asked him to fill in. Working on a Sunday, I said, teasing him. A bad sign. A sin, too. Flying in the face of the laws of God and the church, too. Sure, hadn't the bishops been up in arms about it recently? And they have to have their way, you know, those bishops. Our eyes met. Some of us just have to work Sundays, he said, bishops or no bishops, and that's that. The world doesn't stop on Sunday for everybody. I agreed with him. What would happen if the Guards, nurses, doctors, bus drivers, bar staff, radio and TV people didn't work holidays and Sundays? He was totally right. And even if he wasn't, I still would have agreed with him.

I began to sense that he was shy, really shy for the most part, and not just putting it on. That he was the kind of person you had to draw out of their shell a bit – gently. But he was nice, genuinely nice, and sensible, I thought. Okay, he was good-looking, too, which helped. But that wasn't all. He was growing on me. It looked like we were going to get on okay together … He said that he didn't know anyone here because he didn't frequent the club. I got the feeling that he liked my company, my personality, the way I had about me and, yes, I may as well say it, my body, too – particularly my body. I thought I caught him glancing at my crotch a few times. Was it to see if I was hard? I caught his wandering glance for sure the second time. And he knew. Oh, he knew. And I was glad, even though he looked away into the crowd. Shyness again, maybe.

We shared another round. Talked some more. It was getting late, and I was getting restless. It was time to speak up – put the cards on the table, and ask. I was fairly good at this game. Confident. Believed in myself. I rarely asked anyone, if I wasn't sure of the answer. And tonight, I was extra confident.

Soon the club would be closing – it was nearly two a.m. already. Would he go across the road for a coffee? Sure, he would – emphasis on the word 'sure', I noticed. Brilliant! We exchanged a smile. Hot. I was getting horny again. I was there. From here on in, I was master of the lingo. The rhythmical lingo of the body. Yes, I was proud of my handling of languages, especially my fluency in the warm salty argot of the flesh, the passwords to so many contacts. When someone said they were up for a coffee …

Did I have a car? No. Oh, no problem. He'd see me home

as well. A 'ride' home would be nice, I thought. Where did I live? Southside. Oh, Southside. Even better. He was going that way himself – to his B&B. And where was I staying? My aunt's. Auntie Nora. My great-aunt, really, but we called her auntie. Pity I couldn't afford a flat of my own or a rented room even. Ah well. A real pity. And what could I do about it now? Still, things could be worse. At least we had the car for some shelter. Left to our own devices.

Then we kissed. Our tongues seemed to take over and reach for each other, pressing hard and longingly together. The two of us standing there, right at the bar. Locked together, in people's way and not even knowing it. The pair of us melting in each other's arms, becoming one, almost.

We drove off. The grey city half-asleep that time of the morning – and my right hand pawing away … at his knee, his thigh, his cheeks, his tackle … and him nearly ready to leap out of his skin like a jack-in-the-box as I fondled and fumbled under the sleepy eyes of the city, pulling back my hand at red lights in case anyone looked in on us. He was bursting for it: but what with driving, gears, indicators, and traffic lights, his left hand was busy most of the time, or, at least, it should've been.

Did he know the way? The area? Yes, sort of. We were nearly there anyway. He'd been around here a few times before. He'd find it, all right. Some quiet side street? Cul-de-sac? Or beach? No. He knew a car park that would be empty. He'd been in it once. Next on the right, he thought … That was it. Another right again at the fork in the road …

A huge square car park spread out before us. Was it for a supermarket? Not at all. It was a quiet chapel car park on a back road. They might have thought we were robbers if we parked near a supermarket, but a chapel wasn't worth robbing. He smiled at that. Where there's a chapel, there's bound to be a priests' house nearby, I thought. Maybe the priests would wake up? They'd drop dead if they saw … It wouldn't be fair on a holy priest, especially an old one. We both laughed together at that one. It wouldn't do any harm to open their eyes a bit – teach them about the outside world. But maybe we didn't even have to. Maybe they'd be into secret night-time services. They're probably more used to this caper than we are … if half the stories you hear are true, I'm telling you. Some of them dropping off in private 'bath houses' around the city. Taking dizzy turns. Strokes. Heart attacks. Dying on the job even! Work pressure. On the 'night shift', of course …

He parked the car tight into a wall. This corner of the car park was dark under the shadow of tall trees on the other side of the wall. After the engine wound down, a short silence passed between us. Then a quick look round, just in case. There wasn't a sinner about. How could there be? We both had to get out of the car for a piss. Each of us at either side of the car – me on my side, him on his. As quick as we could. We got back into the warm comfortable car, shutting the doors as quietly as possible, scared of wakening any creature, alive or dead. For who'd be about that time of night or morning, but a thief, a drunk or some other lovers.

Soon we held each other … pawing … petting gently. Some Radio Two music playing soft and low. We hugged awkwardly, squashed against the dash. Usually I could master and manoeuvre such small spaces but I found the front of the car narrow. Could we move the seats back? Sure we could, and from the bottom, too. There was a 'knob' down there, in the middle, between my two legs, or where my legs should have been! There was a tiny wheel at the side, just behind me, if I could reach my hand across. Aah, now that was much better. Far more room.

What a great car, I said. You keep it nice. Some small talk seemed necessary. You must have a good job – an office job, I bet. I squeezed his soft hands. They weren't exactly scarred and hardened by construction work, like my own. I let him rub his hands over my chest and belly, enjoying their gentle touch. I put my arm under his to pull him over somehow to my side of the car so that he could lie on top of me, real close. Our bodies together, mouth to mouth, chest to chest, stomach to stomach. We kissed hungrily. His full, beautiful weight pressing down on me.

And you won't even tell me what kind of job you have, apart from this one, I said, drawing my breath and teasing him. I mentioned the fancy car again. God, you're a strange one. You must get a good wage? He looked at me. A lot more than I'll get for my handiwork tonight, he replied. I liked his way of talking. Or maybe you're married with a wife at home? Oh, sure he was. He'd five or six children at the last count, he said. But they certainly weren't allowed in this immaculate vehicle! I didn't believe a word he said, of course.

We put our arms around each other and hugged tightly. For a few minutes, we didn't move, simply savouring the moment together as lovers and strangers. It meant a lot to both of us. Then one of his hands started searching about, down between the two seats until he lifted something out. I looked round. A small bottle. A bottle of holy water, is it, to throw over the car every now and then for protection?

It's got to be done, I said, taking the poppers that he offered. Now that you've opened the lid, sure ... I took two deep sniffs of it, one nostril after another, and got an extra hot kick right away. All at once the blood went racing in my veins and my heart started pounding like a jackhammer. He took some, too, with a flourish. Oh, so the poor wife waiting for you at home must've got you that bottle; stuck it down into your pocket so you wouldn't forget on your way out? I said, teasingly. She did and all, if she only knew what it was, he said. And we'll need these, too … soon. He pulled out a box of tissues from behind his seat. We'll soon have tears of joy out of you, boyo! he said. Mansize, I said. Good thinking. Next thing we were wrapped in each other's arms again, more passionately than before … it was now or never.

Righty-ho, then. How far was he looking to go? To fuck me, or for me to fuck him? Neither. He was clear about that. He'd no condoms anyway. Why didn't his wife stick a rake of them in his pocket? I'd a few on me somewhere, if I could find them. No need, he said. Okay, if that's what he wanted it … In any case, it was right to be careful – especially these days. So, a handjob. A hand- and blowjob, maybe. 'Come together, right on …' By this stage, he was underneath and I was on top, both of us undressed and unafraid, not even feeling the cold or any shyness between us, the windows all steamed up especially for us, it seemed, by the alchemy of our breath. His soft tender hands made their way between my legs to fondle my prick, gently, stroking and petting over and under as he pleased. Then came lips and tongue – licking, all warm and tickly. Meanwhile I took pleasure, too, in the good handful and mouthful he offered. Each of us with plenty of spunk in us. Then, tensed in bliss, we came in lunges, spraying jets of joy and relief. Both coming together, fit by fit, almost.

It was as well he had mansize tissues, as he mopped up

afterwards. God must have invented them, and him, too, I said. We both laughed out loud, a heart-filled laugh, and lay back again. Soon, it would be morning. We'd get to see the sun dance yet, maybe …

Number seventy-seven, I said, looking out the window. Over on the left – see that pink door? Well, it's not that one, but two down! I'm sorry it's not sixty-nine, but it's not my place, it's my aunt's. No sign of life yet – Auntie Nora must have slept half the night by now. She'll soon be up at the scrake of dawn, though, and footering around the house. I wouldn't be surprised if she drags me out of bed to help her to second mass … Drive on there a bit.

He went two hundred yards down the road before he pulled in and turned off the engine.

My hand was on his knee. He put his hand on top of mine, joining our fingers, gently and tenderly, all the way. I turned my palm around so our fingers were locked together. We squeezed palms even tighter.

Oh, the peace I felt at that moment, our hands gliding over each other. It was like the blood had stopped in my veins. Tonight's lust was nothing to this. Nothing. I had never known such a feeling of calm. I looked into his eyes, my moist palm tight against his. There was a stranger's kindness in that hold. We were strangers lost on a wild night of joy. That was what it felt like. Joy and affection and loneliness all in one. Wasn't there more for me in life than the hunt and the one-night stands? I'd been there, done that, and bought all the T-shirts. Maybe it was time now to give up that lifestyle, free and fun as it could be sometimes … Yes, I wanted more than just some 'action'. I was starting to feel kind of grown up. Like I was a man now. Maybe he was the kind of person I could settle down with, some day, if I got to know him right. He was different somehow from the other men I'd met when I was playing the field and every position on it. My wild oats were well and truly sown. But even though I was still young, maybe I could share my life with someone. A more permanent relationship. It felt like I was wising up. And what did it matter if he was nearly ten years older? Maybe he wanted something more serious, too – for us not to be like strangers when we would meet up again, but to see each other on a regular basis ... in the clear light of day.

But he didn't, which surprised me. Not the fact that he didn't want to, but the way he was so sure about it. Maybe a quickie was all he had wanted, a one-night stand, because he had a man of his own at home. He said he didn't. Would I see him again? Maybe. If he was in town. No promises. He had his arm around my neck, his fingers playing with the back of my hair as he kept an eye on the window and wing mirror at the same time. What about a phone number? Did he have one? Yes and no. He couldn't give it. There were other people at the same number who had no idea. Too bad. Perhaps he really was married! But I'd be careful when I phoned him. I could call at a certain time of day – whenever suited him. Day or night. I would take a half-hour off work if I had to. No, it had to do with business, he said. What business? Okay, then, forget about *his* number ... I'd met plenty like him before. Did he want *my* number? He'd take it, he said, writing it out with a biro from the glove compartment. Between eight and nine was best, week-nights, I said. If I wasn't in, just call back. If he was asked, because of his stranger's voice, just say he got my name from somebody else because he needed a wall put up out the back and needed a brickie … but there was no hurry, and he could call back. He wasn't to mention all that he'd seen already and that it was himself he wanted a job done on. He laughed. Maybe he would call then. Okay, he would … some time, when he was coming up to the city. It would probably be a month or two, but he would call, if he could. He seemed to promise this reluctantly, only because I had asked. I could see him in the club, he said, or wherever else he was. Some weekends I went home myself to the country. But from now on, I was going to be at that club every weekend. I wanted to keep in touch with him somehow or other. It meant that much to me.

We sat in the car another few minutes, saying nothing. Neither of us wanting to break the sacred silence between us. Then a strange feeling of loneliness hit us both, I think. Me, anyway.

Another quick hug before we parted, and we kissed briefly again. Plus one more time for luck, letting our tongues meet for a last stolen second.

Finally, I got out of the car. Slowly. Quietly. The cold air making me shiver. There wasn't a soul to be seen under the streetlamps looking shy and lonely now in the daylight. I took a long deep breath of morning air, all the way down into my lungs. Shook out my clothes. Made sure my belt was done up right. Straightened myself. Then shut the door, telling him one more time I hoped to God I'd see him again before too long.

And so I did. The very next day at twelve o'clock mass – when he stepped up to the altar.

Translated by Frank Sewell

THE MAN WHO EXPLODED

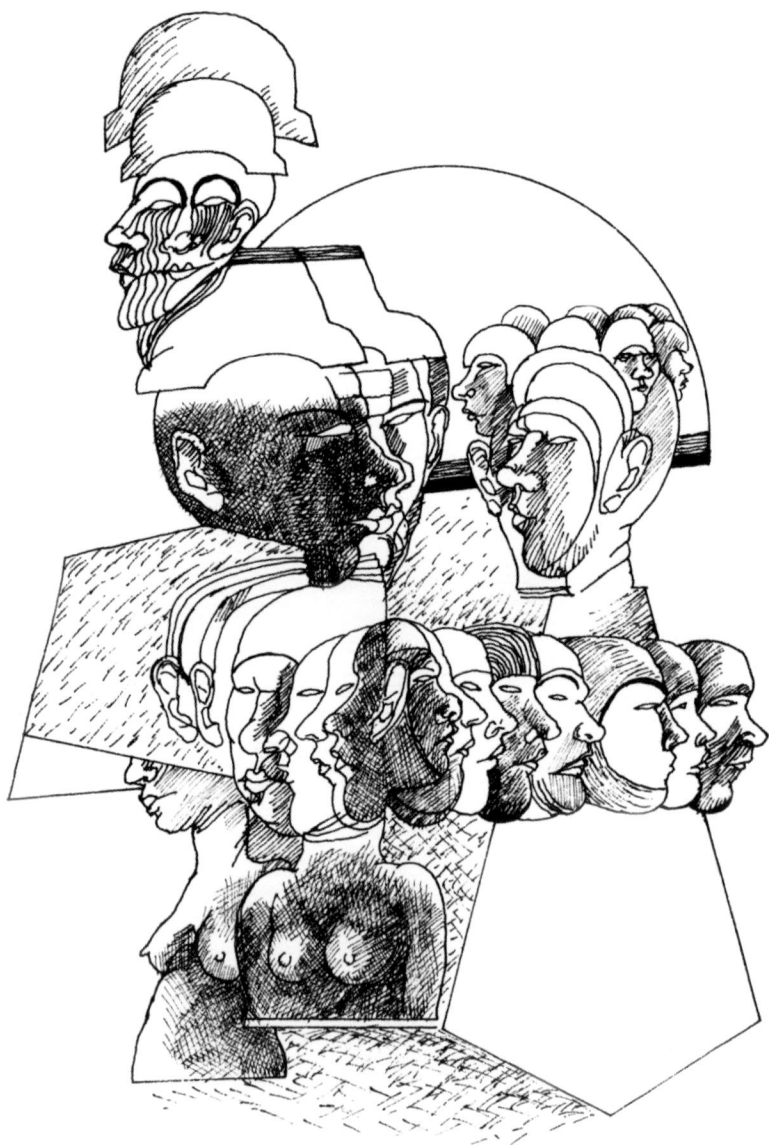

Where exactly did it happen, is that what you're asking? Is it? Right smack bang in the middle of the street, Joe, that was it. Smack bang in the middle of the street. The upper main street that juts out from the square in the guts of the city. Where else did you think? Are you right, or are you right? All the action happens all the time in the guts of the city. He wouldn't have bothered his arse exploding way out in the suburbs, and why would he? That would have been the end of it. No more said. Waste of time.

Saturday afternoon? That's what I said, Saturday afternoon when the place is busy as hell. Shagging shoppers! Shagging shoppers, Joe, with things to do and their shagging kids off school. And half of the hillbillies down from the mountains, with shag all left to do except make some use of their free travel. Finding out who else was in and about. Bad news, Joe, bad news. He picked a lousy time to explode, I'll say that much. He could have really fucked things up, he could have. Standing out there in the middle of the road like a statue. And then, boom! Traffic screwed up for the rest of the day. Traffic jams everywhere. Time to duck, I'd say. It wouldn't have been so bad early in the morning, or late at night, or even on Sunday, apart from mass time …

A warning? What do you mean 'a warning'? Warning my arse, Joe, cop yourself on. People who are going to blow the shite out of themselves hardly give a warning. Why should they? It's part of the game, man, part of the show, part of the miraculous mystery of the big bang. Anyway, if he gave a warning, nobody would have seen him, would they? Nobody there to tell the tale. Everyone fucked off, like snots off a shovel. Fucked off like hares with gas up their arse. Not a twit nor a twat left on the street. What'd you say? Winos? Okay, winos if you like. Winos or quarehawks trying to take the balls out of his eyes or the change from his pockets if he had any ... or the police, or the army if they bothered to come out to defuse him ... and I don't suppose they'd bother. What the hell could they do anyway? What could they do to stop some guy determined to blow himself to kingdom come? Who ever trained them for chrissake? How can you have an expert who knows how to decommission some knob for blowing yourself up? And then what if he went wham bang just when they were fiddling with him, if he got them right between the eyes and under the oxter? The army experts were clueless as well. I suppose they had a lot more important work to do. Anyway, a man isn't the same as a bomb. You're right there, Joe, you could take the harm out of a bomb easily enough, but a man, a person ... even the American Army itself couldn't take the harm out of a person, never mind defuse them. Isn't that why he exploded without warning. Oh, he was a Tricky Dicky all right, slick enough to make no excuses to nobody.

Stuck a pin up his arse, is that what you're saying? I don't believe that. Hate that. They made a hole in his arse with the jab of a pin and he went up in splinters? Ah, come off it, cop yourself on, Joe. That's all balls. Bollix. Pig's bollix hanging down. Don't believe those crap-artists, Joe, I'm telling you.

That's all me eye and Betty Martin. Some chancer made that one up. It's only pub-talk. Bar blather, pub piss-take. What do you mean, everyone says so? Doesn't one thing lead to another, a lie for a lie and a truth for a truth! For chrissake, he wouldn't blow up like that if they made a hole in his arse. Come off it, cop yourself on. Wasn't there a hole there already, there had to be. A hole so big that the sun shone out of it, some people said. But, hang on, that's not a nice story. Forget I ever said it. But one way or the other, Joe, he was a man and not a balloon before he exploded. A man like any other man. A man first and foremost. Even if he exploded because he swelled up like a balloon, he was still a man for all that ...

Internal pressure? Maybe so, Joe, maybe so. Could have been too much pressure. You know what I mean, him swelling up ... expanding, getting bigger, like something boiling, bubbling over and not being able to hold himself. Oh, I suppose you're right, Joe. Had to happen, sooner or later. Gave way at the sides and was ripped apart. Of course he couldn't have stood that goddamn pressure another second. Even a solid stone statue would have gone up under that strain. And booze? Go on, say it straight out, Joe. There's no doubt that the booze had something to do with it as well. Doesn't it always. Drink is always involved in cases like this, wherever there's trouble and aggro, you'll find the drink. But I suppose he did have some kind of excuse, however small. I suppose he did, Joe. Wouldn't things be properly fucked up if he exploded for no reason whatsoever ...?

Did he have a job? Is that what you're asking, Joe? I didn't hear that he had. Is a man a real man if he has no job? They say he had none anyway, that he didn't want one, but that doesn't mean he was idle – some arty-farty thing they say. Messing around with art? Okay, working with art, Joe. An artist if you like, in fact, he was quite an important artist if some of the reports are to be believed. Others denied that, of course. Don't they always. There you have it again. As many begrudgers as you have arse-lickers. Now don't ask me why. I don't understand this caper any more than anyone else. I'm as ignorant as the rest in these matters. But whatever kind of art he was up to, he was always doing … doing queer things. I'm telling ya, really weird things, things that made no sense, things that were useless, some people said. One way or the other anyway, Joe, listen I'll tell ya … this Yank bloke comes to him one day and buys a tree, a fecking Papal cross. Ah no, Joe, forget that Papal cross, that's all shite. Look, you eejit, this one was made out of wire, one he made himself. So this American Yankee bloke buys this tree made of wire, not just any old kind of wire, but shagging barbed wire, imagine that. Barbed wire just like that spiky stuff around a prison wall. Pots of money! Oh you're right there, Joe. What else. They say he got dollops of dollars for his tree of wire, something you wouldn't get for a shagging Papal cross even if it grew. No way José. Now what do you make of that?

Jaysus, imagine having a forest of wire … you'd be a millionaire in a year, a bloody millionaire, man. Somebody said that a wire tree grew in America, that there are wire trees growing all over the place there. Could be too. Now what do you say, Joe? Leave it to the yanks, boy. They'd grow anything, even a bloody strand of seaweed out in space. Now isn't that weird, the great artist's tree of wire. But that's what done for him too. Went to his head in the end. If it wasn't for his art and his wire tree he'd never have exploded. Many trees have fallen, but how many people have exploded?

Too true, Joe, too true. Could be that his head got too big for him. It happens ... happens when people become famous. That's what happened, maybe. The pressure. That's it, the pressure and the fame and all that goes with it. Looking over his shoulder all the time at the other artists nibbling at his arse. It wasn't enough for him to be famous. He wanted to be bigger than the whole shebang of them put together. There they were always before him, haunting him. On the streets. Every corner of the town where you could stand or sit making way for themselves to lie down, thrown down in a dirty heap, as if they owned the place, giving each other airs and graces and rewards, selling themselves and their art before anyone else. All eyes on them, Joe. Huge crowds milling around them from the bank manager to the yobbo – examining their art, praising it as if they knew something about it, saying it was great for them to be there, that they added life to the city, and you wouldn't mind only most of them are only ... only ... piss artists. That's it, Joe, you took the words clean out of my mouth. Piss artists. Don't dirty your mouth again with the word, that's it. Didn't one of them even claim that the stream of piss on the side of the road that his mangy shitty dog did – the one who was always crawling after him – was modern art. He stuffed it down his throat. That's what put so much air in him. No wonder he exploded with spite, to get out of the way of that lump of street garbage, that lot who were robbing him of his reputation for their own glory. Maybe he just had to explode ... just to start again, to get back his own sense of self-worth, to know who the fuck he really was. To make art of himself, every frigging bit of him, that's what they said, to make himself into art ... and then to explode. Without warning, without sweet whack all smack bang in the middle of the city streets. It was then they called what he had done modern art. I'm telling you they did. They accepted him then when they got it straight up the arse, or in the face, whichever you prefer. They had no other choice anyway when he was fucked up in a billion pieces. By jaysus they didn't, Joe. Now they have him all lock, stock and barrel. They can keep him, they can fucking keep him.

And they did. Maybe if they didn't want him when he was alive, they had no choice but to take him when he was plastered all over the place in bits and pieces. Every bit of the city got their own bit up their arse and in the nose and down their throat, when chunks of his fat slob body were fucked around every building site and every arsehole street in the arsehole of the arsehole city. By jaysus, they had to put up with him then, Joe, I'm telling you that – a blob of guts here, a chunk of gob there, a toe or a finger or whatever, a bit of liver splattered on a lamp post, a bit of an ear stuck on to the graveyard gate, a few fingernails half-stuck in the door of the National Theatre, a smidgen of lung smarmed on the goalposts of the football pitch ... perched on the peak of the top of the cathedral one of his balls – that's a good one for you, they hadn't found the second one yet, crowds messing around as if they were on a treasure hunt ... somebody said there was somebody from some American sperm bank sniffing around ... that the blue-rinse crowd of frustrated American women were looking for a good deal. I mean, jaysus, the great artist's sperm! Probably too late, Joe, probably too late. Half his prick shot off on the top of the convent wall ... the only two young nuns in the place pissing themselves laughing, the old nuns shrivelled up in their surprise and good fortune, asking the archbishop to bless the place again from top to bottom and to keep two holy vigils one after the other. A sliver of his heart landed on some bank sub-office, one of his eyes came down smack plop on the Mansion House, just as you'd expect, a gobbet of his arse thrown up on the dole office where he collected his money every Tuesday, a shred of his foreskin stuck to the Garda barracks – they were looking for fingerprints in case of foul play. A wedge of his skull on the roof of the lab of the university, they were drawing up charts already hoping to make some use of them. Bad story, Joe, sad story. Anyway, as for the rest of him, I don't suppose anyone would know the difference, mounds of muscle, bits of bone, blobs of blood, whorls of water, brickbats of bone, strips of skin, gobbets of gollops of dollops plastering whole segments of the city, street- and lamp posts, and telephone boxes, and bus stops, and zebra crossings, and advertising hoardings, and shopfronts, and schools, and statues of martyrs. You'd hardly say that any shagging bit escaped, Joe, nothing at all, only maybe a bit of a backstreet or a hole of a public toilet, certainly some of the women's toilets escaped they said ... maybe he was a ladies' man, after all ...

Some queer sight. The way they left him there. Even the dogs of the city weren't willing to go near him. They weren't willing to go near him even though their guts were hanging through their balls with hunger. I suppose an artist's cantankerous flesh, especially one who exploded, isn't the same as everybody else's mortal flesh. Dogs didn't eat nothing after that, no other meat. Some wag said they were becoming veggies, going around with their noses in the air, like snobby shites.

It was said, of course, that he should be put back together again. They could stitch him up, they said, if they got all the pieces in one place. Maybe the government could squeeze some slush fund European grant and get some unemployed FÁS people to, like, stitch him so he'd grow together again. It was said, Joe, it was, but what else hasn't been said ... A small oriental little fart of a doctor up in the hospital who might be able to blow some life back into him. He's miraculous. Maybe yes and maybe no ... Sure thing, Joe, but I'd put my money on the second, maybe. Maybe they should have tried it anyway. You never know. But they didn't. No more than Humpty Dumpty in his day. The bigwigs of the Corporation voted unanimously against it. It was said that they did it out of fear ... they were scared shitless that he'd wreck the joint if he was alive again. And anyway he was worth three times more scattered around the place dead. But between the two of us, there was even another reason, Joe. Insurance! Millions of euros in insurance that could never be claimed if he was alive again. That's one for you! But that wasn't the official version, of course. The Corporation scumbags said that it would have been unfair to the artist. It was his own decision to blow up at that particular time and place – that he was opening a new chapter in the story of art in the city, and, of course, in his own inimitable personal style. A conscious pre-planned decision, they said. A climax all of his own choosing. Some people would do anything, Joe. Sometimes they would ... looking for recognition and publicity. His name in the next edition of the *Guinness Book of Records*. And wasn't he finally recognised in his own native city as a result? Isn't that something in itself? Twice refused the Freedom of the City during his life, and now he gets it, despite the lot of them, with a bit of violence. That was it, boy, that was it. All he ever wanted from the beginning, if they'd only have given it to him ... Recognition ... Exhibition ... A Grand Exhibition ...

A live grand exhibition of himself – and he dead! Hundreds of pieces of art that couldn't be valued, nor bought nor sold because they were priceless. There they were presented to the city. Real modern art, Joe, the genuine article, made from his own natural resources. The Junior Minister for Arts, Culture and the Breac-Ghaeltacht was summoned home from his sunny holidays to officially open the exhibition – while the stuff was still fresh, they said. Ordered home, I'm telling you, he was. Accompanied by government officials, just in case. The Minister said that the entire city outdoors was now one gigantic, ornamental gallery. That no developer or demolisher could touch a brick of a building from now on. Now, wasn't that worth it! His fame spread far and wide beyond these shores ... great tourist potential and money-spinner for the entire region. Would bring thousands of interested visitors ... he said it, Joe, he did. Double-decker buses full of tourists disgorging themselves into the shops. Small Japanese with their hand videos. Fat-arsed middle-aged American women with their spyglasses. Tall blonde German beasts with their cameras clicking. Trained guides showing them the city from open-top buses. It's true, Joe, leave it to the tourists. Would be easy to satisfy them. Or to fool them. But the experts, Joe, the experts! They're the crowd to watch. Standing on one another's toes trying to make sense of it all ... Every specialist and expert in the country, in the world, if it comes to that, pathologists, psychologists, pseudologists, sociologists, anthropologists, geologists, gayologists, arseologists, pissologists ... After all, it isn't everyday that someone just blows up. Wasn't that what they said. Everyone for himself making sense of it in his own way ... research for some of them, lectures around the world for others, money-spinning books, television appearances. More guards needed twenty-four hours a day, or they'd cream off whole blobs of him in little plastic bags as samples ...

Is that true, Joe? They're going to build a monument to him? Jaysus, that's a new one. Nothing to stop them, of course. And why wouldn't they? Just across from where he blew up on the edge of the square? The minister allowing twenty thousand euros already from some special fund nobody knew nothing about until now? And the church matching them euro for euro? Two church collections and a special big collection at the church gates every Sunday? How's that for ya? How's that for ya, when you think how short we all are of money. Maybe the Pope himself will come to Ireland again to unveil it? The holy Joes trying to claim him as one of their own now, are they? A martyr to the cause. They'll make a shrine to him underneath the monument, thanks to the Corporation. They'll canonise him yet, will they? A cardinal or an archbishop on his way from Rome researching the case already. Then we'd have our own saint. We would, Joe, if you like that kind of thing. People being cured. Rumours going around that miracles were about to happen, just to be patient ... any day now. Keeping an eye on people in wheelchairs and other invalids sentenced to death by disease. The clergy claiming that all the bits were holy relics. The nuns would have to stop their perennial prayers and come out of their convents to feed the hungry hordes coming on pilgrimage to the shrine – their backs broken stuffing them with chips and hot dogs. A string of rent-a-loo cabins like a rosary around the square to be kept sanctifyingly white for health reasons. Overflowing, despite the charge for their use. Nice fat profits accumulating for the nuns to be spent on the black babies.

What's that, Joe? You didn't see the guy who exploded? That's bloody odd in itself. Everybody else saw him, even people who weren't there, people who weren't even in the city that very day. They saw him, I'm telling ya – or at least they said they did. Unless of course they saw him on television that night, it was on all the news bulletins – and then they thought they were there, that they actually saw him go up in bits. You know the way it is, Joe, memory playing tricks with people, especially nowadays, virtual reality and all that. Too true, Joe, too true. So it goes. There are people and they'd see anything at all. They're there though. Drug addicts and junkies. People shooting themselves up, day and night. They'd easily see someone who exploded, even if they were never there themselves. Now you're talking. Druggies would see anything – Puff the Magic Dragon living by the sea and floating off somewhere over the rainbow. They'd swear black and blue that they did. And there'd be worse fools who swallowed their story. Who'd be first to believe it, Joe ...

But I'm horrified to think that you of all people didn't see him ... a sensible guy like you who sees everything and wouldn't let the grass grow under his feet. I have to say I thought you saw him, that everyone saw him ...

Absolutely. Isn't that what I say all the time, Joe. Don't

see anything you don't want to see and is none of your business. Keep your nose clean. It'll be seen anyway, despite yourself.

But you'd recognise him anyway, if you spotted him, wouldn't you? You mean you're not sure? What do you mean you're not fucking sure? I'd be amazed if you didn't recognise a guy who exploded – much the same as any of us really, except he's blasted into tiny little bits. I find it really strange to think that you didn't see him, Joe ... really and truly. I was sure that every Tom, Dick and Harry in this city saw him. Except myself.

Translated by Alan Titley

JUNCTIONS

'Will you pull me off?'

Out of the blue, he said it. Right into my ear. His breath warm, moist almost. I didn't hear him. I didn't hear him at all really. Didn't catch what he said or so I let on to myself.

I grabbed my pint, I could feel myself burning up. I took a gulp. Another. And another. I ran my tongue in a circle around my lips, and heard a welcome grumbling deep down in my guts. I could feel the cool drink going through me.

'Great pint, this is. And your Guinness looks good, too. You could tell Gabriel pulled it. He pulls a good pint, not like the other young fellas.'

He took another long, greedy gulp from his pint and turned back round to me.

'D'you hear? Do you hear me, boyo?'

His voice was getting louder.

'Yes. Yes, I do,' I said, afraid he would raise his voice any further. 'Sure, can't the whole place hear you?' The pub was packed, and I knew most of the ones there; some better than others. A fair few of them worked at the same factory as me.

'*Will* you pull me off?'

He sounded more gentle now. I pretended to cough. Once. Twice. Trying to drown out his talk if he wasn't going to shut up. Finally, I cleared my throat.

'It's my round,' I said, getting up, even though I had half

a pint in front of me. 'I'll get one in for last orders.' I walked over towards the bar. 'Get me a half-one as well,' he shouted after me. 'The night is long ... and cold. We'll have to keep ourselves warm.'

'Yeah, right.' I didn't even look back. I felt a sudden hatred towards him. Real hatred for the dirty bugger. Why the hell did I have to sit beside him at the start of the night? For a chat, maybe. A chat about football. Every single goal or foul in every game, every penalty kick in the last few years gone over again in slow-mo by the pair of us sitting in the corner for two whole hours. And there was me thinking I knew the man better than that. I did. I mean, I thought I did. He was always about the place.

I tried to order a drink, but couldn't get served. So I just leaned my weight on the counter like I didn't care how long I would stand there. Maybe if somebody else turned up, I thought, I would have a good excuse to get away from him. I bet he was looking at me at that very moment. Staring, gawking. His eyes going right through me, racing up and down my spine, all over my body, working out my height and size, comparing me to other lads he has had, probably. Sure, isn't that what they're like? Isn't it? Or is it? The same way I am with the women, probably.

'Pint of lager over here and a ...' Gabriel didn't hear me. Or if he did, it made no difference. I didn't mind. I would be back there sitting in the corner all too soon. I would rather have been cornered in a boxing ring than hemmed in there. But, unfortunately, there was no one in the pub to intervene or call me aside. No one as far as I could see. Everybody was busy talking to somebody else in conversations breaking out all around me. Were they even listening to each other? I couldn't tell. God, if only Róisín wasn't back at college! She would have been here for the weekend. And didn't he know rightly that we're together? If only she were here tonight, I thought, I would have had proper company. But I had come in on my own.

'Good on ye, Gabriel. A Guinness, please, a pint of lager and a half-one.'

Finally, I had got through to him. Gabriel sighed, under pressure, saying that there were a few orders in ahead of mine. I didn't mind. It gave me a chance to think.

I would have to get out of your man's way, somehow. Find or make up some excuse. He had a fair few on him and was already half out of his head. He would disgrace anybody. Disgrace them in front of the whole world. Disgrace me in my own village. And him one of them, too. The dirty devil. How many others had he tried it on with already? People round here must have known for ages. I would have to steer clear of him from now on. Who would have thought? Training the football team as long as I can remember. Involved with our own under-18s this year. Everybody praising him to the skies.

'Isn't Little Jimmy great, spending all that time with the young lads,' they said.

'Isn't he football mad … training them ten years since he stopped playing himself.'

'Over on the pitch with them every day of the week.'

'Sundays, holidays, in all weathers.'

'They could go even further next year.'

'They could be county champions.'

'They would have won last year only for the ref.'

Out on the football pitch every day. The eyes must have

been bulging in his head, waiting and watching over us as we came in and out of the changing rooms. None of us suspecting a thing. Not me, anyway. And him peeping at us, posting up training schedules, announcing the Sunday team, going round collecting the jerseys, kindly tending to anyone with a knock or injury. 'Everyone into the changing room now for the team talk.' Couldn't he have done that outside? Not him; that wouldn't have suited him. I used to wonder about it, but he always liked to say his few words in the changing room, walking round sometimes with his fist clenched, encouraging us, giving off to someone who wasn't on form – and the whole while running his eyes over us, fantasising, perhaps – and all those times we went into the showers, naked, having a laugh sometimes. He must have been there watching us, me especially, maybe, since he had picked on me tonight. But that's what they're like, guys like him, aren't they? God, I was blind. Blind.

'A Guinness, a lager and a half-one.' Gabriel set them in front of me. I was about to stick my hand in my pocket but he was off again.

I was for home after this round. Better to keep out of the way. Far better than hanging round here much longer. Tonight, anyway. Especially if I was stuck with him. There was a match on tomorrow, too. So I would be as well going to bed early, I thought. The best thing I could do was just go home. Definitely. I mean, as long as your man didn't try and follow. That would be the worst, if he came after me. Followed me on the way home. Attacked and hurt me. Compared to him, I was a lightweight, too. I could never beat him – big and stocky as he was, quite fit for a man of forty-five. He could be dangerous if he wanted to be. He could do some damage. I probably wouldn't be able to play tomorrow. How could I explain that one?

'Twelve sixty-nine,' said Gabriel, arriving back. I paid him. He turned quickly on his heels, and brought back the change. Steadily, I headed back to the corner. A pint in each hand and the half wedged between them and my fingers. He was sitting there quietly, thoughtfully, staring at me, his legs stretched out. He had lit a cigarette and was blowing smoke rings, wide ones, in the air. He looked like he was in a dream, watching them disappear as they drifted closer and closer to the lights above.

I set down his drinks.

'Knock that back,' I said to take the dodgy look off his face. Then I set my own pint down.

'That'll put hairs on you,' he said, looking over my pint, 'and a wee stir into you, too.'

'The music's great tonight,' I said. 'There's nobody like the Anchors. Have you heard their new one about the potholes?'

'*Potholes!* Never mind the potholes, boy. Have you ever heard "She's Your Mamó"? She's the one with the pothole! And did you ever hear what happened to her?'

'Yes, often. It's a great song.'

'She's your Mamó, fucked with a pole,' he sang. 'She's your Mamó, the hag with the gold ...'

'That's not the way I know it.'

'Who cares what you know? Who's talking about you?'

'All I said was that's not the way I know it.'

'Way! I'll be having my way with you soon enough. Ha ha!'

He was talking right into my ear again. He laughed, a deep, dirty laugh.

'Don't say anything yet. Just knock back that pint and we'll get there in no time.' He put his hand on my knee. Left it there, and laughed again, slowly and drunkenly. I could hear my heart pound with hatred for him.

'Take your hand away. And don't fucking mess with me, one way or the other.'

'Och, sure doesn't everybody like a wee bit of fun sometimes?'

'I have my fun with women.'

'Women? Sure you're only a young fella. A young fella who still hasn't dipped his wick yet in the fires of the flesh, eh?

'It's fuck all to do with you. But I'm old enough and big enough, thank you very much.'

'Big enough for me, too. Just a feel. No one will find out about it. We'll soon have another wee ball game going between the pair of us.'

'Fuck off! I'm not one of those. Go find one of your own lot.'

'My lot? Where are my lot around here?'

I turned away from him. I had to get away right now. Get offside somehow as soon as I could. Find some excuse. I took a quick gulp of my pint, got up and headed for the jacks. At least I would get a couple of minutes away from him in there. Maybe he would cool down a bit, change his mind, listen to me, and fuck off. God, I hoped so, or that someone else would come and sit in my place. If only they would, I thought, that would be a great excuse for getting shot of him. Whoever sat there was welcome as far as I was concerned. I would just lift my pint and join some other company without too much bother. No one would notice a thing.

I had hardly got my dick out when suddenly he was behind me, squeezing my thighs.

'Fair play to you, son. Fair fucking play to you.'

He slapped me on the arse. Even though I kept looking straight ahead at the damp wall in front of me, I knew he was looking over my shoulder.

'Fair play to you, son. We'll beat the shit out of them tomorrow.'

'Aye. So we will.' He was making me nervous. 'But you'd think you'd let me have a piss in peace. So stop it, will ye?'

He was stroking my buttocks.

'Piss in peace, eh? A lad having a piss looking for peace. Peace! Next thing you'll be wanting a soft seat to sit on for your wee piece ... or is it a big piece? You and your peace!'

'Fuck you, man!'

'Shake well after use, so they say.'

'Cut it out!'

'You should really shake it more than that, they say. Did nobody ever tell you?'

I couldn't even finish my piss with him there. Why the hell didn't I go into the cubicle? God, if anyone came into the jacks and saw us there: him trying to grab hold of my balls, me trying to keep him off, twisting away like a rugby player trying to make a getaway from a scrum.

'Stay away from me, you cunt!' I said. 'You'll pay for this!'

'You know very well I'm not going to hurt you. But I can't help the way I am, can I?'

'That's as may be for you; but it's got nothing to do with me.'

I swung round, pushing him away at the same time. After a short struggle, I made it past him to the door.

'I'll see you soon on the way home and ...'

I didn't hear the tail end of what he said. If anyone had heard the bastard ... Better be on guard, I told myself.

I decided to have a game of pool, even though I'm not great at it. But at least I could get away from him that way. I lifted my pint and went into the back room where the table was. I didn't bother looking back; hoping to God he wouldn't follow. I set some change on the edge of the table.

'I'll play the winner,' I said, since there was no money down already.

'You needn't have bothered placing that there,' said Dara Dic Dharach, half-full of drink and of himself. 'One more second, and I'll pot this black, no problem.' And so he did. I shoved a euro coin into the slot. The balls made a long loud racket as they fell. I lifted them out in twos, letting them tumble into the triangle.

'Your break,' said Dara when I stood back. I took the cue. Broke. Powerfully. The balls scattered and rolled all over the table. I soon won. We played a second, third and fourth game, until we were chucked out at the end of the night.

Outside, a dirty drizzle was falling so I zipped my anorak right up to the neck and headed home. It was stupid to stay so late. I should have left earlier when it was dry. I really should have, but what else could I do when I had to wait for your man to clear off? Thank God he wasn't shadowing me, I thought, or following me out the door with his oul talk of 'I can't help it. Let me hold you. Just for a minute. I won't hurt you.' The dirty oul devil. And why the hell had he picked on me? Did he think that I was like him? Don't tell me ... Jesus, no! It was bad enough if he did. The things people would say about me if they heard ... And, anyway, why would he have thought that about me? I was the last one to spot that he was one of them. Did many people know about him? No, it was impossible. Incredible. There would have been talk. I would have heard some gossip or rumour about it, definitely. One of the lads would have brought it up at some point, when they were drunk, if nothing else. The story would have been all over Gabhal na gCloch in no time.

But then again, maybe not. Things like that were never talked about in public – only in whispers – that is, if they were talked about at all, apart from the odd stray hint. 'There's none of my lot about,' he had said. He would know; he had probably spent plenty of time hanging around to find out. Aye, but if he was up in Dublin or some other city, he could have a quare time of it there. A rare oul time. He would get to know his own lot, all right. Find ways of mixing with them. Of getting acquainted, friendly or whatever it was he wanted. He would be ten times better off there than stuck in godforsaken Gabhal na gCloch, looking for something he couldn't get. But who knows? Maybe he was as well where he was. With everything changing. AIDS spreading. People like him in danger. In Dublin especially, there was always a chance. But surely there was no AIDS in Gabhal na gCloch? Not yet, anyway. Or so you would think, in a place so remote. But who could say for sure? All kinds of people, these days, were staying at the hotel and summer homes: American, English, French, German. The campsite was right next to Jimmy's land, too, and the place was full of Gaeltacht students from the summer on. The locals running after them. God help us, there was no knowing; you couldn't be sure of anything now. Still, Little Jimmy couldn't have AIDS, for God's sake.

But I would have to avoid him anyway from now on. Definitely. No matter what happened. Steer clear of him. Only trouble was, what if the bastard was on the road like he said. Letting on that he was just standing there waiting for a lift home? He would be bursting for it by now. Out of control, maybe. Ready to stop someone, and attack them, maybe, if they didn't give in to him. He was not one to be crossed. The number of fights he had got into playing football! He had never walked away from trouble before, and was well known for it. And didn't he used to be a boxer? He could really hurt someone if he wanted to. And what could I do? He was far stronger than me. If he got worked up, he could attack me, beat me, half-kill me. Or rape and kill me.

Perhaps it would be better to give in to him, I thought. Cooperate. Do whatever he wanted so that he would go easy. No! That would be dangerous. The best thing would be to let on you were giving in, and that he could do whatever he wanted. Open his trousers and pull them down gently, slowly, then give him your trusty kick in the balls, and make a run for it. Leave him doubled up in pain. Better that than hang about for a battering. After all, I was slim, but I was fit and fast on my feet.

But maybe I wouldn't have to do anything. Maybe he had met someone else who had taken him home, or maybe I would meet some neighbour on the way, and walk home with them?

But I didn't. There was nobody on the road. There wasn't a sinner, nothing but far-off headlights beaming on and off heavenwards in villages across the way. All alone, I hurried along a mile of road in the dark and wet. Every now and then a dog barked, shattering the silence for a moment as I passed certain houses on the way. The dogs seemed to aggravate each other, but were too lazy, it seemed, to follow me, or to get wet, probably. A deadly silence fell once more and spread over the countryside as I took the narrow road at the junction.

'There you are,' he said, leaping out from a hole in the hedge. 'I've been waiting for you for ages.' He stood stock-still in front of me now, his half-open belt hanging down. His arms were stretched out to grab me and there was a strong smell of drink off him. Suddenly, he rushed at me, grappling, nearly knocking the breath right out of me. About to fall on the back of my skull, I looked him right in the eyes, my stare as hard as an ice pick going through him. The closer he got, the more I inhaled the strong smell of drink off him. I tried to raise my knee.

'Fuck you … you dirty old cunt,' I gasped.

In the dark sky over my head there wasn't a star to be seen.

Translated by Frank Sewell

AT THE STATION

The station – which had never gone anywhere – was tired. Not tired of travelling, of course, but tired of staying put. It would never take a single step, not even a step back or a sidling sidestep. No wonder then that its limbs were stiffening, cramping quietly.

If it could only stretch itself out ...

If it could just once indulge in a long, groaning stretch from the bottom of its spine up, ribs and limbs shooting outwards ...

Then, to crown that, a long deep yawn ...

A yawn that would send air rushing in and out of its congested black lungs ...

One lively breath that would spike its stagnant blood with crystal clarity ...

If only it could, maybe then it could revive itself ...

The dirt. The dry, grey concrete walls. The heaped piles of rubbish. The black film of grime. The dust. The street-muck of shoes, feet, soles, clinging in an encrusted layer. Empty cans kicked by unseeing feet. Plastic wrappers blowing about. Yellowed cigarette butts, the odd one with a bright lip-print. Smudged ash. Spilt, sticky liquids. The acrid smell of the years. Greasy chips. Crumpled remnants of ticket stubs that would not be used again, that held no further hope of journeys, not even of a wild goose chase ...

But the station had to stay still, set, right where it was. Stranded. On the southeast of the old city that had grown out of it. Beleaguered. Powerless to move anywhere in spite of its great bulk. Not able even to nip across the road for five minutes. Facing outwards in all directions. Scores of rails flowing, stretching like rays out of it in every direction, like spokes from the hub of a wheel. Each one of them a free agent heading away. Looking like they're trying to escape from the station. Voyaging out. In a hurry. Speeding up of their own accord once they're out of sight. Taking to their heels, full steam ahead. As if they're taunting the station, saying, 'We're off, you do what you like.' Leaving the station in the lurch, standing cold, empty, abandoned, like a young man jilted at the altar.

The station was miffed at first; felt they were making little of it; making use of it. People. People walking on it. Making it suffer. Tearing through it like a whirlwind. That's all they wanted, to rush right through. People foisted on it. Just their hurried footprints. Not so much as a half-ounce of their minds. Not a heartfelt beat of their love. Not a flash of their spirit. Not an inch of their hearts. Not a cry of joy, or barely that. Rushing, hurtling, dashing. To be in the station was a trial to these people. They hated it; thought they would never get out of it. Giving out about how you'd get lost in it sometimes. Going up and down its corridors. Badly laid out. The signs weren't clear enough. They'd send you the wrong way. There should be some straightforward way of getting through it. Through it and out again, once and for all.

And the station felt their reluctance; tasted the sour tang of their delight at leaving. Their poverty of spirit. As if they were spending their last ounce of time in it. It was an irritant and they were like animals lashing their tails to get rid of a horsefly on their flanks. The long, drawn-out queuing in impatient lines. Compulsive glancing at blameworthy watches. The poor decent watches, you'd think it was their fault, that it was they who were keeping time marching on, making people lose out on the next stage of their lives. Delaying them. Looking at the backs of each others' heads, into each others' ears, leaning their weight on one leg, looking up noses, into mouths and then squaring up as if to say, 'What the hell are you looking at?' Smelling the sweat off each other. Watching themselves being watched and stepping back, uncomfortable and embarrassed, whenever glances collide. Looking again. Everyone in the queue ahead judged guilty by those coming behind them. The boredom of it all. The futile waiting that breeds resentment. Breaking out sometimes. Hostility taking over their thoughts, blanking them out. That time of day when their imagination, their creativity, their regard for their own lives, is at its lowest ebb. Everything reduced to rushing and running, to a mechanical leave-taking. Often the leave itself not even properly taken. No real goodbye. Just tooraloo.

The station was loneliest at night. The great push homeward over. Utter desertion. It missed the chatter and bustle and buzz. The silence giving way to endless reflection. Forcing endless reflection. The only comfort; thoughts of other stations far away that this station knows exist. Those with their names branded on their gates. The crowds rattling down the rails towards them. Stations. Brother and sister stations who can never be company for this one, because of the rigours of geography. All it has by way of connection are tentacles of knowing extending in their direction; its only handshake with them happens through miles of rails.

Company.

For all anyone knew, then, it could have been the station itself that invited them in in the first place. Took them into its arms. To its bosom. Encircled them. Took them under its great wing like a broody hen with a flock of lost ducklings.

Company. They were company, weren't they? The tramps were in no hurry, had no business to see to. They hung around the entrance area during the day, but the inner area was theirs at night till bedtime and beyond. Loitering about from pillar and post, that was their occupation. Lazy, idle loafers. And they thought highly of the station, their bed, their roof, their hearth, their common room. Their welcoming shelter from the wind and weather. Cradle for their noisy dreaming.

But as the years went by some middle-aged men slipped in past them. Quietly, furtively, evasively at first. But regularly all the same. More and more often. Getting gradually bolder, more confident. Sometimes a few, sometimes about ten. Up to twenty the odd time on very busy nights ...

And the station recognised the shadowy features of every one of them. Very seldom was there a strange face among them. But, now and then, there was. And when there was, it soon became known, became familiar, bit by bit in the protective darkness. They walked very carefully, these men. Quietly, except for a comradely whisper of talk that wouldn't wake a child. They kept walking, walking slowly. Around. Slowing down. And around again as if keeping to an irregular circle that was marked out only in their imaginations. Stopping silently, regularly for a minute here and there. Staring ahead like a Christian quietly making the Stations of the Cross. In and out of dark, blessed, secure corners.

And the station welcomed them under its gentle skin. They were its sprightly, loving company in the middle of the night and the small hours of the morning. It had made a stronghold for them in the back, at its southwest corner. Beside the wall in a place where an old storeroom had been, with a broken door that you could get through from two adjoining streets outside. An old storeroom. An old storeroom that was barely in use anymore, that was more a liability than a facility. Full of cobwebs, and insects, alive and dead. Bats too. Nothing going in or out there during the day except once in a blue moon ... a relic from the dark days of coal and smoke. Nothing packed away there now except old rusty machinery that would never come to life again. Scrap.

And the station saw the men make their own of it in the grateful darkness. Saw the warm affection they gave in the station storeroom. The way they knew every corner of it, every square and crevice and niche. As if they could see in the dark like cats. And the lonely station welcomed them. Enjoyed their eager arrival, their lack of haste, their appointments and intentions, their easygoing good nature. Their company, the time they had on their hands. It welcomed the deep desires of their hearts and bodies. Their hidden loneliness. The gentle respect they showed the station until they left at first light, before dawn. They were its lifeblood ...

But people began to talk. The station heard them. Big

bold headlines written large in the newspapers that were sold noisily at the entrance gates of the station. The station read them itself with its windowy eyes. It was criticised, condemned ... They said it was an old station anyway, that its heyday was over, that it was dangerous, that it was an accident waiting to happen, that somebody someday would be injured or killed if something wasn't done about it immediately.

The Garda Superintendent spoke out also. Politicians spoke out. The clergy spoke out. News editors and radio broadcasters. The great and the good spoke. The people spoke. The people who spoke were heard.

One winter morning before daybreak, the menacing machinery rolled in, arrogant and masterful. One of the bulldozers started attacking the old shed, tearing it down, pushing and pulling. Another machine came and joined in supportively. It wasn't long before a whole crew of machines were rampaging, advancing in a noisy threatening line like an army going to war.

The city's pedestrians stopped for a minute or two as they passed, to look on. Transfixed by the sight. One or two of them gave a silent cry of approval. 'Thanks be to God,' some of them said and, 'It's about time,' before going off on their own assured way.

Half a dozen tramps gathered as well, idling the day away across the street, watching, seeing wall after wall reduced to crumbled dust by the big iron claws – facing the fact unwillingly, stooping, huddling close together. The odd passer-by noticed, sensed their loneliness, their brokenness, their loss.

Up on the slope of a blind alley, south of the station –

where they had their own vantage point – stood a handful of middle-aged men. Still and silent, like men waiting patiently outside a wake house for the body to be brought out. People going by barely noticed them. But they could see the destruction from where they stood, could smell the dust on the tainted air they drew into their nostrils, could hear the stubborn clamour of the work pounding in their ears. The devastating lunges of the bulldozers. The aggressive boring of the drills. Hardly a word passed between them, just a stray syllable now and again, as they stood grouped together at the side of the sloping street.

From time to time, in spite of themselves, against their better judgement, they would take a long lingering look at the debris of the station. The sheltering walls that had accommodated a treasury of private moments in their lives, broken. Still they stood their ground there in a brave semicircle right to the end. Staring and staring. Men without refuge.

Translated by Katherine Duffy

THE MERCYFUCKER

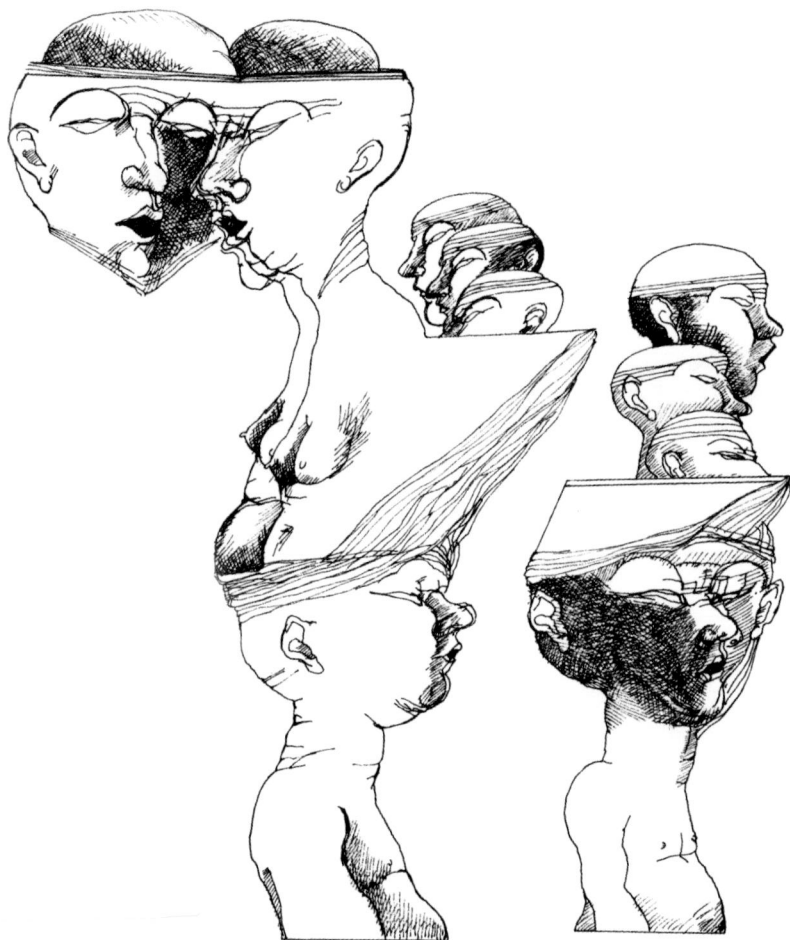

A Mercyfucker, that's what he said he was. Sitting on the low wall of the square with a can of cider in his hand. Mercy. Fucker. I considered each word separately. I hadn't a clue what he meant. I knew what a motherfucker was all right, but mercyfucker, that was a new one on me. A merciful fucker, I said, in my own mind.

I looked him up and down again. A young, handsome boy, certainly. Very handsome. Barely eighteen, if even that. Small but strong-looking, hard-muscled. Short dark hair sprouting from the top of his head like little birds' tails. I'd never have called him a fucker. I sat down beside him.

A Mercy-fucker, I say, after a brief pause, and it was obvious from the slow way I pronounced the two words that I didn't understand what he meant by them. He blinked a few times, involuntarily, as if the sun had got into his eyes. He looked at me like he was wondering where on earth I'd sprung from.

There's a group of us, he said, who spend time around the square here and we fuck men who are cruising. We do it for mercy's sake.

Mercy, I say, love of God and love of your neighbour free-associating in my head, though I couldn't hope for too much of that in the middle of London. I wanted to laugh, but I don't think he'd have known that from my voice.

Exactly, he answered. That's exactly it. For mercy's sake. We only service old men and middle-aged men. A lot of them are pretty wrecked. Not handsome or good looking. Those that wouldn't stand much chance of having sex with other men. That type. Do you know what I mean? We do it as an act of love for God.

God's compassion, I say, as a statement, not a question, trying not to let my amazement show. Out of compassion, he said. And for the love of God. There are so many poor devils that are gay who never got a chance when they were young and who've lost their looks now, he said. A lot of them went through tough times in life. Some of the old-timers never even met other gay men when they were young, never mind get to know them or have a relationship with them. They were just left with a huge gap in their lives. Now they hang around here, lonely for a life that's gone by – not the life they actually had, but the life they never got to have. The life they never experienced and they're full of regret that they're not decades younger.

The young man stopped talking for a minute to take another sip of cider. His story was still amazing me, especially how steadfastly he believed in his vocation.

There were about ten of them in the group, he said. They had come together to try to do something for those who had suffered in life. He described some of them. How they would take him back to their flats. How some of them craved the company just as much as the sex. The loneliness that plagued them. The gaping hole in their lives. The pleasure and relief, however fleeting, that he was able to give them. He mentioned one man he had met from somewhere in a remote part of Ireland, who was fifty-two. Fifty-two, he stressed, and he was still a virgin – a virgin until I slept with him! Can you believe that? Imagine what sort of life he must have had. Trapped at home on a farm, taking care of his parents until he was over fifty. Imagine being that age before ever being touched with love, or held affectionately. Haven't some gays had, or don't some of them still have, an awful life, he said. Fifty-two years old before he lost his virginity – whereas I lost mine happily at twelve. How did that poor thing manage for all those years?

He was speaking fast. With passion. He took another sip of cider. Belched once or twice and didn't excuse himself. He looked at me as if sizing me up. I looked around the square.

So that was the mercy he practised, I thought. Offering his body and his kindness freely to these men. There was no payment, he was at pains to point out. He wasn't a rent boy. Not that he had anything against rent boys, but that would go against his conscience. He had his own conscience, he said then, and he felt obliged to obey it. That was why he tried to show kindness to people who hadn't been as lucky as he had. And what about people who were in a very bad state, I ask, thinking of some of the bent-over old men that I'd seen loitering around the toilets, some of them withered and sullen, crushed under the heavy burden of the years. I close my eyes, he said. We have a rule: never refuse one of our unlucky older brothers. I close my eyes, I dream of my lover and I get on it.

Then, draining his can of cider and tossing it into the waste bin beside us, he said briskly that he had to go. He stood up. I suppose there's no chance with you then, I said, half joking, half in earnest. There is, he replied. There is a chance with me, but not for you, and he was laughing.

You're too young, he said. A teenager! Way too young, and too good looking too. I'm sure you won't have any trouble picking somebody up. When you're forty years older or more and have one foot in the grave, you can fall back on some mercyfucker out there then. You can be sure the likes of us will still be around. But what will I do till then? I say, self-pityingly. Do you see that old man over there? he said, nodding in the direction of a bald old man standing with his back to the wall of the public toilets across from us. Take him, he said. I've had him several times. He's very easy to please. You hardly have to do anything for him. Just let him suck you. He's a lovely guy, no harm at all in him. A bit backward. He's been waiting there for about a quarter of an hour now hoping one of us will come along. He won't know you're not one of us. Tell him you've just joined up.

Thanks a whole lot, I say, but he's not my type. Why don't you look after him, since you're the mercy man? It's supposed to be your job. I can't because I have another appointment right now, he says, checking his watch. I go to see an old man in his flat once a week. An ex-soldier who lost a leg and the fingers of one hand in World War Two. A mine exploded near him. The poor man's life was ruined. He was only seventeen at the time. He hadn't even been in the army that long. And he's been a cripple ever since, the poor guy. It was a bit strange and awkward having sex with him at first. Being in bed with someone with only one leg and no fingers on one hand takes a bit of getting used to ... but, he said, heading off, you can get used to anything. This is my good deed for today.

I suppose it is, I said to myself, watching him walk away. I was disappointed. My gaze lingered on the way he walked.

But if he'd lost his cock in the war as well, then where would you be? Aren't there plenty of ways to show God's love to others?

But someone else's gaze was lingering on me now. The old bald guy. Still standing nervously at the toilets. His back to the wall. Looking all around from time to time, but in between looking steadily at me. A kind of pleased expression on his face as if he was grateful to see me, as if God had sent me his way. I had a good idea he thought he was looking over what was his, that he was certain now that I was a mercyfucker too, since he'd seen me talking to the boy. Certain that I was here to show mercy to him.

What'll I do now? I asked myself, watching him start to cross the road at the zebra crossing. He was limping, dragging one foot after him. He could do with a stick. Seventy, if he was a day. He looked like he could drop dead any minute. I'd be afraid he'd die on the job. What would I do with the poor, miserable devil? I didn't want to offend him. Imagine if he died in my arms. He certainly couldn't do me any harm, that was for sure, even if I did decide to go with him, but the thoughts of it made me feel sick. I couldn't. Not ever. Never. How did that mercyfucker manage to do his merciful deeds? I asked myself. How did he sleep with someone like this. It was only then that I really understood how compassionate and generous what he was doing really was – there wasn't a shred of beauty about this wrinkled old man, not to me, anyway. I didn't think closing my eyes and getting on with it would do much good either ...

I stood up just when he was nearly upon me. I could look the other way before he got to me, and head off. Hoping to God that he wouldn't let out a screech or start shouting after me, so that people would start looking at us. He could be a nutcase for all I knew. It's not as if anyone would recognise me here in the square, but ...

Come on now, he says; a little happy, kindly smile on his face. Just walk after me. I live at the head of the road. We'll only be five minutes.

I recognised the accent straight away. It gave me a start. He was looking back over his shoulder at me as he finished talking. Although my heart was pounding and although I was sorry for him, in a strange way I wanted to laugh too. I didn't know why, and I felt guilty for it. The poor thing was so sure of me. He was going to be so disappointed. I started walking after him, wishing he'd turn his back properly on me ... Maybe then I could turn and slip away on my own without him noticing, since it looked like he wanted to keep what was happening quiet as well ...

Thinking too that I could walk a little way behind him, that I could take three merciful steps in the direction he was going before I turned away . . . like they do at home when a funeral passes. The three footsteps of mercy. One, two, three.

Translated by Katherine Duffy

THE MAN WHO NEVER LAUGHS

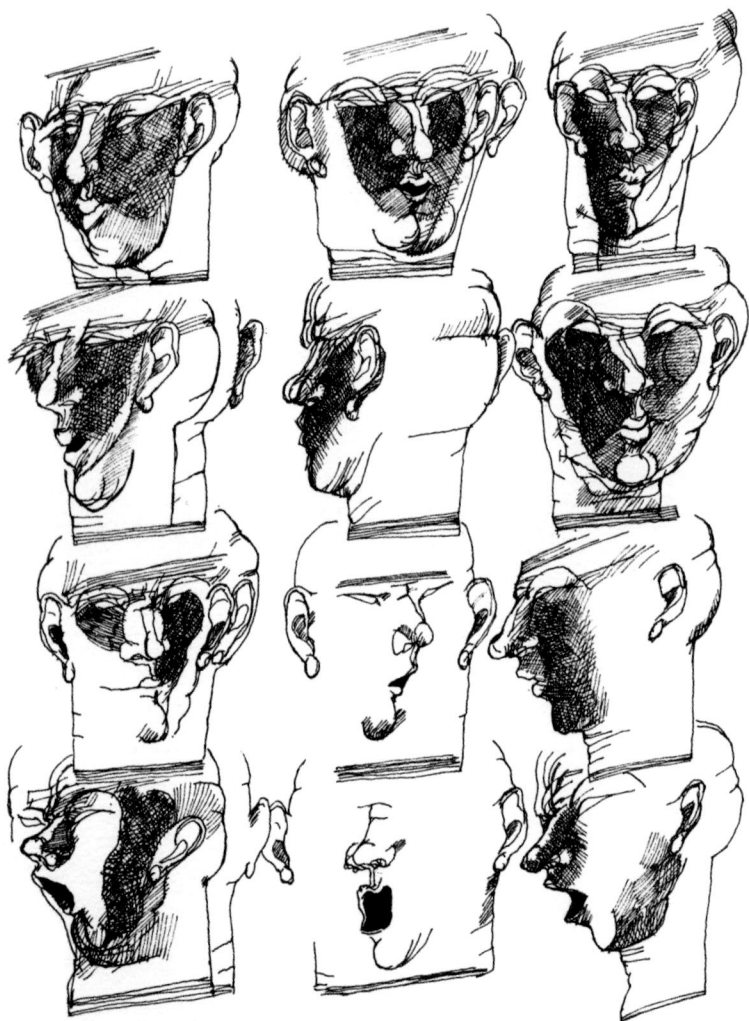

With all due respect to present company, I don't believe that there's any truth in the theory, or any proof of it, that he spent the best years of his life working alongside other Connemara men in London, cooped up in a dark hole, cleaning out sewer pipes that were overflowing with shit, blocked, doing work that no Englishman would do. That it was those years of rotten filth that clogged his laughter, or stunted it at any rate. In those days the stink was everywhere, surrounding him, a hot steam rising steadily upwards, travelling not only towards his nostrils and up his nose, but into his mouth as well, into that little chapel tucked between his eyes and his chin, if ever he laughed or even tried to. Knowing well, probably, that he couldn't laugh or even chuckle without drinking in the mucky filth from one of those great gaping pipes ...

As I said, I don't think that particular piece of folklore is true. I think there has to be a more everyday and reliable explanation than that for his lack of laughter. Weren't there plenty of other men – women too, indeed – cleaning out the very same blocked pipes, and did that stop them laughing? Huh. Not on your life. Most of them were laughing their heads off at all that shit and at the work they were doing. Remarking that English shit was the most precious you could find anywhere under the world's hard surface, as they counted up all the crisp sterling notes that were slipped to them surreptitiously behind the backs of the queen's tax collectors, just for bending over their shovels. But of course, though it's probably not true at all, it's the most popular theory about the man who never laughs – which just goes to show that the human race prefers a well-turned lie to an unpalatable truth. It just goes to show that the more elaborate the lie, the better it travels and the fatter it grows, and not only that but every Tom, Dick and Harry will get another little bit of mileage out of it.

But no wonder, plenty of other reasons were cited for his lack of laughter ... that he had bad breath that would be sent too far abroad if he laughed; that a chunk of apple got stuck in his throat and was embedded there; that he was half gummy or that he had a rotten tooth he didn't want to show; that he believed you couldn't have a politically correct laugh any more, without offending some section of society; that he didn't want to bring on crying from laughing; that he wanted to go easy on his face muscles so that his skin wouldn't be too wrinkled when he got older; that he'd had braces wired to his gums when he broke his jaw in a scuffle when he was young, so his laughter was suppressed even when everyone around him was in stitches, his guffaws squashed out of shape and all mixed up. Trapped in a stale tangle inside him as if they'd been lumped together and caught up in a net.

But wait a minute now. Things aren't anywhere near that simple. Wasn't his mother always insisting that he was roaring laughing in the womb before he was born at all? She was sure of it. She could see him with her own two motherly eyes and, although she couldn't actually hear the chortling inside her, she could feel tremors resonating outward from him through her body. Anyone who didn't believe her only had to look at her stomach and they'd see how much worse her stretchmarks were from all the laughing he did while she was carrying him for so long ...

And wasn't he laughing away still when he was being born, his father swore to it? And he should know, since he was there at home when the child was being born. But then again there was no other witness except himself. And didn't all the sceptics and naysayers reiterate again and again, after that, that the baby had been born feet first. That he had struggled and tumbled awkwardly into life, two or three months overdue. With not the slightest desire to come out at all, as if he was trying to avoid anything to do with life, the tears, the music or the laughter of it all, for just as long as he could – until he was almost able to crawl out into it himself. How could he have been laughing when he was being born, they wanted to know, when it's natural for every living being – as opposed to a stillborn child – to scream and cry with pain and fear and terror, let alone someone who appeared on the scene all shaky and reluctant, falling arse about face into life? Someone like that couldn't have been laughing – or if there was any bit of a laugh there at all, it must have come out of his behind. A farting travesty of laughter, that's all someone like him would produce, they insisted. Sneering at life like that before he even knew it existed, never mind tasted it. Was it any wonder he couldn't laugh properly now. God had sent him an affliction like that in revenge. Laid a cross on him that would soften his cough. He wouldn't be so cheeky again after being taken down a peg or two like that.

There was rhyme and reason to God's revenge, that was the general opinion. After all, was there any worse punishment in this tedious life than not to be able to laugh at least occasionally – and more especially not to be able to laugh your own laugh? To take a good solid fit of laughing, or just to let a little stray screech bubble up from the depths of your heart, after hearing a joke or seeing something funny. What state would that leave a poor devil in, to be forever on the verge of exploding, suffering like a eunuch unable to reach a climax, knowing that the best part of sex was always out of reach, that he could never ever come?

Others believed that he had laughed too much when he was young and that's what had banjaxed him. He was never taught how to laugh properly, punctually, in an orderly fashion as the occasion demanded. Or if he was taught, he never managed to learn, too thick probably, or worse than that, maybe he learned the wrong kind of laughing from continual bad practice? Manky laughter. Faulty laughter. Hollow, holey laughter. A poor, pale, boring excuse for a laugh that never managed to blossom into a good full-blown laugh, no matter how hard he tried. Instead of laughing he made disgusting creaking noises. Some said it was more like a rusty door creaking, and that his jaw would need lashings of oil just like the hinges of a door before he could laugh again. Others compared it to the hoarse croak of a frog, as if the laugh was stuck halfway down his throat and could neither go down nor come up. The loud bray of an ass, that's what it reminded other people of. It was more of a fierce, twisted bray turned in on itself, they said, instead of coming out naturally – and that he was left in the end with neither a laugh nor a bray, but a dry mongrel yelp somewhere between the two of them that would mortify the biggest ass in Ireland if it was unlucky enough to let a sound like that come out of its mouth.

It was generally believed that, as for every shortcoming there had to be a reason, a basis, a fault that caused such bad laughter, whether it be from birth, nature or nurture. The schoolmistress got her share of the blame for all her cross threats when he started school. 'Stop that giggling,' she warned, 'or you'll be laughing on the other side of your face. I'm sick and tired looking at you and listening to you,' and she put him standing in the corner, face to the wall. He wet his trousers. He shrank into himself, so they say, like a slimy black slug when you stick a thorn in it, curling back into its own thick, curved cavity, knowing he couldn't run away ... while all his classmates roared laughing at him.

The big boys at school were blamed as well, for picking on him because they thought he was odd. They'd grab him by the scruff of the neck when they were all out playing in the schoolyard, stick his face in the mud and wouldn't let him lift his head out of it until he'd let out one of his silly snorts of laughter. They had great sport after that looking at the weird, wrinkly print of his laugh in the soft mud.

The parish priest got a good slice of the blame as well, whether he deserved it or not, just to keep in with the trend. He had caught him, if you can believe it, in the back of the chapel during mass openly ogling the thighs of three girls who were on their knees in the seat in front of him. One, two, three, up she goes, he chanted ... stand up ... sit down ... and he would lift up their skirts with one hand and try to tickle their buttocks, sniggering away under his breath all the while ... until the big priest came up behind him, grabbing him by the scruff of the neck one Sunday when the chaplain was saying mass. 'I have you now,' he shouted 'I have you, you cursed bad-mannered little blackguard. Laughing in the

House of God, before God's holy altar! I wouldn't mind if it was a decent, glorious, sacred laugh itself, but such careless, insulting, sloppy laughing ...' as he dragged him up the side-chapel and into the sacristy ... There are about a dozen different versions of what went on there, but to make a long story short it was said that the priest's curse only added to the general faultiness of his laughter.

At a funeral of an uncle of his when he was a young teenager, another uncle gave him a right clout on the jaw. It was all because of a neighbour's dog. The dog had wormed its way through the crowd in the graveyard while they were waiting for the priest to come and lead the prayers. He lifted his hind leg – the dog did – and nonchalantly directed a lordly stream at the back end of the coffin as dogs do in their dignified doggy manner, though not normally on coffins with corpses inside them. Of course plenty of others there were laughing as well as himself, but they were sly enough to hide it, drowning their laughter deep down in their stomachs, below their ribs, under their skin, and, worse than that, managing to look aghast at the shameful, scandalous thing that was happening in front of them. They all squared their shoulders and arranged their faces into masks of impatient disgust until such time as the dog decided it had given the last drop of its dutiful offering, and was ready to make off, relieved and happy, on the lookout for its next point of interest ... But didn't your poor man burst out laughing gustily when he couldn't hold it in any longer and the uncle clipped him hard around the ear, so that the laughter took on the tone of an agonised yowl, the like of which was never heard in any graveyard or garden before or since.

Was it any wonder, then, that he tried to learn to laugh

properly, tried to retrain and rehabilitate his way of laughing? They say he spent hours and hours on his own, locked into his bedroom practising his imperfect laugh, trying to tame it to the way he wanted it, trying to adapt it to his own voice, to his own style. They say he had a tape recorder and that he used to tape himself, trying to laugh this way and that – at different pitches and speeds sometimes – listening carefully to the playback trying to perfect it, as he thought; believing, or so it was said, that his laughter would improve if only he kept working at it.

Practice, practice and more practice. It is thought that he got guidance from some American university that runs courses in Laughter Studies, and it transpired that he got a lot of help from his local TD, who lent him his public relations staff to coach him in laughter presentation skills. He practised on his own a lot as well, it seems. He would often head out alone to hills and mountains off the beaten track, away from all human company, to where the deep glens threw lonely echoes of his laughter back into his mouth, correcting him by repetition.

This annoyed certain people, though. They thought he was laughing at them. They were sure that it was they themselves, more often than not, who were the butt of his jokes, something that needn't have bothered them so much if they had only known what was really behind his laughing. They moaned and complained that he gave them a pain in the arse, a pain in the stomach, the way he went on. They said he had secret laughs that had never been heard before, but that he would let out involuntarily, at the wrong time. But maybe their problem was plain envy which made them uneasy with him, like the kind of annoyance people feel in a pub when a huge laugh erupts from a crowd nearby, falling tipsily on their ears, unwelcome and unasked for, and they feel ostracised by this rootless laughter that's been forced upon them? And every sort of excuse and extenuating circumstance was made for him. Some even said that he was trying to free himself from laughter, to get clear completely of the duty of laughter which is ingrained so deeply in the flesh of every human being. Some thought he was striving to lift all limits and restrictions from his life. Trying to transcend them so that he would never again be under an obligation to laugh, and especially not a false laugh, like those cheesy grins people put on for the camera, or the perfunctory, mechanical chorus of people listening to a joke, whose laughter sounds like the brush strokes of a scrappy broom, especially the ones who didn't get the punchline at all, but who still laugh eagerly in spite of that, trying to be good company ... wantonly wasting laughter that could have been hearty and honest and good.

So who can say of the man who never laughs that there isn't some method in his madness? Maybe he's cuter than the ancient devils of hell. Maybe there's rhyme and reason to his pattern of laughter and maybe he's better off for it? He's so careful not to produce the wrong laugh at the wrong time. Who on earth is to say that his spirit and soul aren't in line with Mars or some other planet out there – a planet where laughter doesn't exist simply because its inhabitants follow their own intuition and way of life and are just as happy for it, maybe?

And why then are people always wondering about this? Wondering about his dark magical ability to laugh or not to laugh? Wondering if he's in touch with fairies or beings from some other world? Passing around stories like the one told by the mountainy man who was minding his sheep when he heard him laughing those skewed, supernatural laughs, and not what you'd call proper, clean laughter from the heart, as he understood it. He says that he tries to compose new laughs every day of the week, that he has composed a series to release at various occasions in the future, as he thinks appropriate, that there are rumours that he will perform them jokily all together some night, in a public laughter recital out in the open air before curious crowds. His own strange version of every kind of laughter since the first time a chimpanzee laughed when he stood up straight for the first time, proving to everyone that from now on there was no need for someone to go loping about like an animal frozen in the position of somebody sitting on a toilet bowl. It was said that all he had to do now was to create a catalogue of his laughter, small snickerings, huge guffaws, explosive giggles, hearty laughter, bitter laughter, once-off laughter, laughter in the face of danger, vivacious laughter, dry laughter, sardonic laughter, insulting laughter, the laughter of the damned, mad laughter, mocking laughter, deafening laughter, sensitive laughter, light-hearted laughter, uninspired laughter, feeble laughter, laughter that turns to tears, infectious laughter, the ghost of a smile, loving laughter, slack laughter, budding laughter ... laughter that misses its mark, laughter that does neither good nor harm, ambivalent laughter, stifled laughter, half a laugh!

He believed he was particularly skilled at the half-laughing. He believed the most accomplished performer is the one who only half-laughs, because half of every laugh is still in the making and that's why he holds one side of his mouth in a restrained grimace to stop the other half of the laugh emerging, to avoid completing it ... and then it's no harm at all for him to laugh and jeer at everyone else.

Keep away from him, he has the devil in him, said one expert after doing some research and studying what he was up to. Satan, the fallen angels, his immediate family and his legions of relations above and below the ground. The expert concluded that he had made a pact with them, a conspiracy against mankind and even against God. That he had sold all his laughs to the devil or given them on long-term loan, lodged them in a locked vault in the Allied Devils' Bank where they will stay until the eve of the last day of the world. That he had sworn solemn oaths that he would not laugh one genuine laugh of the laughter that's allowed to him until that day when he can buy his own soul. That he doesn't want to laugh before then anyway, that he's saving himself, denying himself. He insisted that a person's death throes are played out, inch by inch, in every laugh that's laughed, their final agony, and that people are in danger of exploding from laughing. That the true laughs of this life are on the way out, and that this man who never laughs is putting them all on hold for some big occasion, stashing and stowing them in heaps and troves so as to fling them out heartily on the Day of Judgement when every sort of laugh will be in short supply and the human race will pay dearly to hear even the faintest echo of the tiniest hint of laughter you could hear or feel in your heart. So that he alone will have the most enormous last laugh. The laugh of laughs. All to himself.

Translated by Katherine Duffy

WHATEVER I LIKED

He asked me if I had ever used a shotgun before. I told him I hadn't, and if I was clumsy with it, then so much the worse for the person I'd be using it on. There's no law that says murder has to be tidy ...

Now that I've been convicted by the court and received a life sentence, I have plenty of time to think about things like this. The horror of it. I have all the time in the world, except for whatever portion of it I can manage to fritter away in this narrow little cube of a cell where they have cooped me up. It's all my time now – and that's the damning and the saving of me all at once – even though they tried to take it away from me. I might as well tell the truth now, at this stage of my life, or some bit of the truth anyway. Just as it comes to mind.

'Are you guilty?' the judge asked. I remember that part very well.

'How do you mean "guilty"?' I asked him. 'What sort of question is that?'

'Are you guilty of the crime that you're accused of here today ...' He looked down at the sheet of paper in front of him, as if hoping for some silent support from it. 'That you murdered your parents on the fourteenth of March?' I don't remember what he said the rest of the date was.

'You couldn't call that pair parents,' I said.

'That's no way to talk in a court,' the judge said, a hard edge coming into his voice.

'It's the only way to talk about those people.'

'I'm asking you one more time. Are you guilty?'

'Guilty of being alive?' I say. 'I am. If that's a crime I'm guilty of it. I am, your honour. And those two you mentioned earlier are even guiltier of that crime, too, if we accept that it is a crime.'

I remember I gave a big long statement then with a passion that surprised even myself. Maybe 'statement' isn't the right word. It's too official a word, too legal sounding. I made a speech, I suppose. A speech that wasn't all that coherent, or maybe that was coherent enough at the time, but I can't seem to put the sentences together right now, so many days later.

Let the Son of God be the first and the last to judge me, I say. Sentence me to death, and he can pass a true verdict on my whole life from the unlucky night I was conceived, a judgement free from prejudice and bias. And I remember someone shouting out then that there was no death penalty in this country, more's the pity.

'More's the pity,' a second voice echoed in support ...

'More's the pity,' a third time, I answered, or retorted, to be precise.

'Even a blind man can see he's a nutter, a complete madman,' a voice hissed from somewhere else in the room ...

Where was I? Oh my birth. Yes. It all began with my birth, I say out loud. It was all wrong. I was born to those two after their bit of grappling ... or to that woman, I said then, correcting myself, since he had taken himself off to the ends of the earth by then, as per usual. That birth should never have happened. That birth was a bad start, ruined everything else, it was nearly the end of me. An ill-fated birth.

'Here's some breakfast for you, if you want it,' says the middle-aged warder in his light grey uniform, hunkering down to shove the tray under the iron grating of the door. That's about all I get from him, apart from hearing the rustling tread of his footsteps as he walks away. I stare at the brown tray with its white bowl of porridge, its plate of scrambled egg, two reddish-brown sausages, a couple of crisp slices of bacon. On a smaller plate beside it lie two slices of half-burnt toast, a pat of butter wrapped in mocking gold-coloured paper. In the corner of the tray sits a cup of black coffee, with a little tub of milk lined up behind it, waiting. It's there if I want to use it. Two white cubes of sugar lie under the handle of the cup. I get a whiff of breakfast smells as I lift the tray and put it down on the little square table that's only just wide enough to hold it. A mix of different aromas at first, but the hot coffee smell is the strongest of all. My gaze falls on the plastic armoury of knife, fork and spoon ...

I lose interest in the food all of a sudden, just as soon as I pick up the fork. As if something's stopping me. Something inside me telling me not to eat it. Not to touch it.

One day when my father came to see me he brought me an apple that tasted of fish. An apple from out of his pocket. A soft yellow apple that tasted of fish. I like fish, but when I take a bite out of an apple, it's the taste of apple I want. It startled me. That's why I threw it at him, after taking just the one bite out of it. A bite I hadn't chewed. A bite that I spat out rudely, in a temper, my face roaring red.

'Now, now,' my grandmother said, coaxingly. 'This is your father. You have to be nice to your father.'

'Sure he's no different to anyone passing by out in the street,' I said ...

My grandmother had a flat three floors up and so I had a good view of all passers-by. Those flats were knocked down a long time ago – there's a swish hotel there now.

And nobody could believe I had done it. At first anyway. Until they started bringing out the evidence. He wasn't someone who would commit a crime like that, a lot of people declared. A quiet fellow. That lad was well brought up by his grandmother. Lad, I thought ... Eighteen years ...

'Could any family member commit a more horrible crime?' the judge asked.

'They could, your honour,' I say. 'What about forcing a book on someone who can't read. Except a picture book, of course.'

He called for order in court then because some people had started to laugh.

'Amn't I right?' I say. 'There aren't too many pictures in that big Bible of yours, now are there, despite all its thin transparent pages.'

My father gave me a hundred euro that day. He said it was from the two of them. A little present from the two of them, he said. They had got together to celebrate the day with me in the hotel. Their long-lost son.

'Neither of us had any idea what you might like,' he said.

And how could they have? As if there was any need to say it.

'If we give you money you can buy whatever you like. You're all grown up now, God bless you. You're a man. You can do whatever you like. Make your own way.'

You'd swear it was him who had raised me, and that I

was just taking my leave of him, that he had reared me and was going to miss me.

'So you see, your honour, he told me I could do whatever I liked. He gave me that freedom. Didn't he say I was grown up? Wasn't it he himself who gave me the money. Who said he didn't know what I liked or what I wanted but that I would know that myself. I would know what I wanted.'

'What you're saying makes no sense at all.'

'What I'm saying makes a lot more sense than my life does. My life doesn't make much sense, maybe, but there's some sense in what I'm saying in this senseless life.'

Now I notice the reddish-coloured sausages on the plate across from me. I'd forgotten about them for a while. I pick up one with my spindly fingers and start to eat it. It's cold, gone hard and greasy. I eat the second one and one slice of the cold toast. I drink the bitter coffee in two gulps, shaking my head involuntarily at the black taste of it. It gurgles its way down through me. I put the tray under the grating of the door. The warder will collect it later on. Maybe he'll chat to me, stay and make some remark about how much or how little I've eaten ... or maybe not.

It was when I realised that they were going to sleep together again that night, that I went out to buy the gun. That was what made me lose it altogether. I knew I could get one from a guy that used to hang around the alleyways. If he didn't have one on hand he could get one for me within the hour. But as it happened he had one. He took me to a derelict house and pulled a board up out of the floor of an upstairs room. Ninety euro. I had ten euro change out of my father's hundred. He loaded it for me for that price. He asked if I needed more cartridges. I told him there was plenty in it, that I'd only be using it the once. He asked me if I had ever used a shotgun before. I told him I hadn't, and if I was clumsy with it, then so much the worse for the person I'd be using it on. Serve them right.

'You killed two people,' the judge said. 'Even if there were any sense to your ravings, even if you thought you were entitled to revenge, why did you have to kill both of them? Why tear two families apart! They both had young children! You left two more people widowed.'

'What has to be has to be,' I say.

'Even if you insist you didn't want the life they gave you, that doesn't give you the right to take two lives in its place.'

Would a judge say something like that in court? You wouldn't imagine he would. He'd hardly say something like that out loud, even if it's what he was thinking. Maybe now that's not exactly what he said at all … Or maybe it was the lawyer who was talking at the time … I see now that I could be getting a bit confused again – maybe the description I'm giving isn't all that accurate, if I was to write these thoughts down some other day of the week. But the bones of the story are sound, not like my own tired, sore bones. I'm certain of that. Isn't that enough, after all? The overall picture is right, pretty much. Sure what do the niggling little details matter? … just like it hardly matters whether I say the cup on the tray here beside me has tea in it and not coffee … as long as there's a cup there. But to come back to what the judge said when he said something about two people. Two.

'Since I didn't ask them to give me a life I didn't want, then didn't that give me the right to take their lives?'

'Two people. Two.' The judge said 'two'. I'm positive of that much.

'To be fair,' I said, 'if I had half-killed both of them, that wouldn't have been the same as killing one of them completely. Even after half-killing they'd both be alive. Wouldn't they? That was the problem.'

'The problem!' The judge said the word. He repeated it a few times from his high desk, his eyes popping. I still see those big eyes, popping like two white, hard-boiled eggs.

'They had a hand – if that's the right word – if not a say in creating me,' I say. 'They share the responsibility, half and half. Someone like me wouldn't happen to be here without the two of them working hand in glove. I'd be doing an injustice to both of them if I discriminated between them. Half and half, that's the way it was. Side by side they stood. It would be unfair to the one who was put to death if the other one was left alive. It would be unfair to the one still alive if I'd killed the other one. Wouldn't it, your honour?'

The judge didn't answer me. He had his arms folded, like someone listening because he had to, but who wasn't really hearing me. In one ear and out the other.

'It's the same whichever way you look at it,' I say. 'My conscience wouldn't let me act any other way except the right way, the kind way. Be kind to the people you meet in life, even people you don't know very well, that's what my grandmother used to say to me when she was alive. She's dead a long time now. You never know who they might be or what sort of dealings you might have with them in the future, she used to say ... How do I know whether or not they had planned to spend the night together in the hotel? I don't think they had – I think it was just at the last minute that they decided to stay with each other. It had been two years since they'd last met before that ... and before that again who knows how many years. And both of them with young families at home.

'What I wanted, your honour ... what I wanted was to avoid them replicating me. I happened so easily, so simply, like something that sprang up overnight. I did. And it was part of my revenge to make sure that the likes of me wouldn't be cast on to life's stormy waters so casually again ... just for the likes of them. For their temporary relief. Them and their shenanigans. Their gratuitous pleasure. Having sex without a second thought, without paying the price. That's all they wanted. Sex without strings, without consequences. But everything has its price.'

He asked me if I had ever used a shotgun before. I told him I hadn't, and if I was clumsy with it, then so much the worse for the person I'd be using it on. Serve them right. There's no law that says a murder has to be tidy ...

They're fast asleep now, and I've just tiptoed into the room. This is the moment. They look so peaceful, lying there by the light of one of the bedside lamps that they've left on. Her head on his breast, her dark hair tossed loosely all around her. Her face completely visible. His right arm is around her, under her breasts as if supporting them. His left hand cradling her head. I think to myself it's a strange way to fall asleep, the way his left hand cups her head. The smell of drink. I didn't realise it would be so strong.

'And after all that you stole the money that was in their pockets,' the judge said.

'I didn't steal it, your honour.'

'Wasn't it found in your possession?'

'It was.'

'Well if it was found on you, didn't you steal it?'

'The money found on me was my own money, your honour. They were dead, your honour, weren't they? As the legal heir to those two that was my money. I only took what was mine, your honour. Isn't that the law? Your law?'

The state pathologist said they died almost instantly – from bleeding from the brain. Bleeding that started from the shot at point-blank range that they each got. He couldn't tell who was hit first, or who died first, but there was very little time between them. Seconds, he reckoned.

For quite a while I couldn't make up my mind who to shoot first. It didn't occur to me, when I took the gun out of the deep pocket of my coat, that this was a decision I'd have to make. Lack of experience, I suppose. If I shoot him first, I'll be strong enough to deal with her, if I have to. But I'd be afraid she'd start screaming and yelling the place down, and causing a big rumpus. Everyone would hear. That's how it happens in films. He wouldn't be like that, I don't think, if I shoot her first. More likely he would try to do something to save his skin. As I raise the gun I realise now I have to make a decision and aim at one person before the other ... before I aim at myself maybe.

I didn't see much blood. And nobody said a word. I heard little choking snorts. Gurglings in the throat. Do you know what I did then? I put the point of the gun on the light switch – that had caught my eye – and put the light out, leaving them completely in darkness. Goodnight, my parents.

I hear the warder making his way back to me, pushing his creaky trolley ahead of him as he loads up all the trays. Stopping, pushing on. Following his routine. Since I'm in the very first cell inside the main door, I'm the last person whose tray he'll collect. He'll be off out the big iron door then ... Out ... Out.

He still doesn't know how much of my breakfast I ate and how much I left for him to take away. Just as that pair didn't know what kind of end was in store for them that night. Just as the state pathologist doesn't know which of them I killed first. Just as the judge doesn't know whether I was sane or mad at the moment I pulled the trigger. Just as I don't know where I'll be tomorrow. Yet.

Translated by Katherine Duffy

STOPPING FOR LUNCH

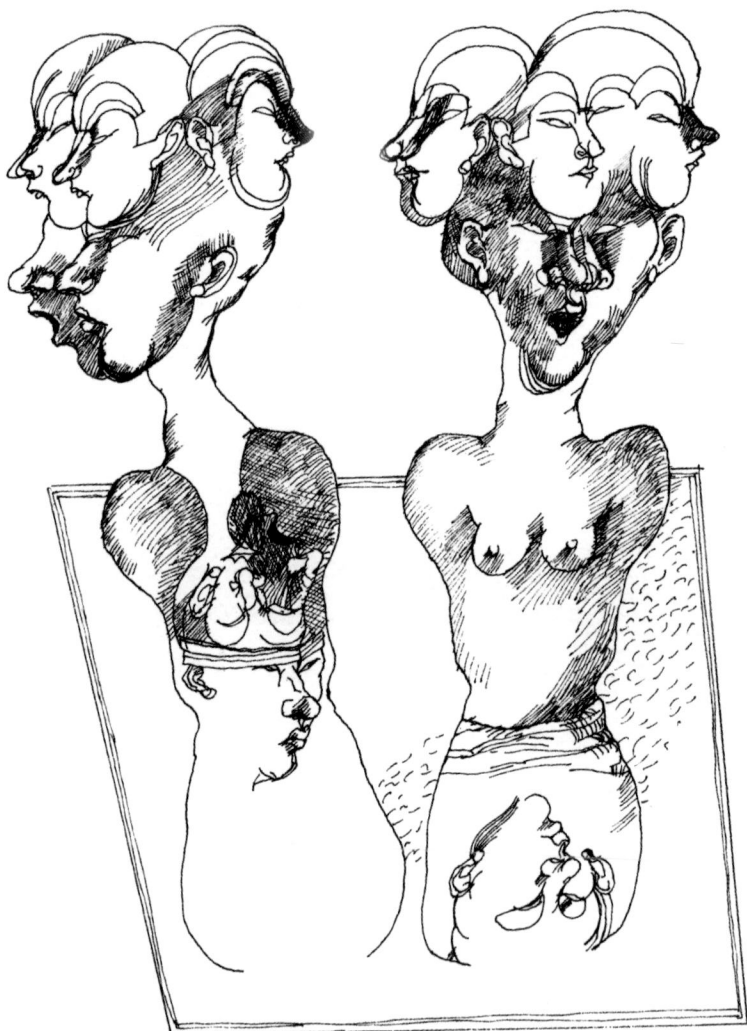

I was coming back from the shop with my little bag of groceries, my bad leg slowing me down, trying to rush at the same time so I could let the wife get away out to work. The kids, you know how it is … can't leave them on their own just yet.

I was on my way home from the shop, as I said … on my way there … when I heard strong, quick footsteps behind me, gaining on me like a squall of wind until whoever it was was breathing hot and heavy at my shoulder.

'You're going the wrong way,' he said. That was his greeting. Then he stood out in front of me right in the middle of the road, having sidestepped me neatly, nimble as a dancer.

'Am I now?' I say as if I couldn't care less. Maybe, I said to myself, he didn't recognise me at first, or maybe he was half-cut or maybe he just didn't realise I'm from the North Village. The youngsters that are coming up now, you know … The best thing was to keep on walking.

'Didn't I just say you're going the wrong way?' he said, more emphatically this time. I didn't know who he was or who his people were, but I guessed he was from the area all right. I should be able to recognise him from his father or one of the old fellows who lived about the place.

He grabbed hold of my shoulder suddenly, getting a good handful of my jacket.

'Haven't I just told you you're heading in the wrong direction?' he said a third time, an edge in his voice now, and he pulled me over to the side of the road. 'Is there any use in talking to you?'

I stepped back a bit from him when he loosened his grip. I could feel my heart beating faster. I shrugged my shoulder like I was shaking off the imprint of his hand and straightened myself up.

I looked him up and down, trying to figure out who he was. He stared into my eyes as if he was waiting for an answer or for something that would give him an excuse to start into me. I spoke quietly, since I didn't want any hassle or trouble, keeping a tight grip on myself. Knowing well from his strong, manly physique that I'd be no match for him.

'I'm only going one way,' I say, 'and that's the right way.' My voice was still level. 'Look, that's my house down there!'

'Oh so that's where you hang your hat, is it? Maybe you'd be as well off not living there anymore?' he said, lowering his voice to a fierce whisper. I knew he was a nutcase, but I couldn't help it. There was something nice about him at the same time, something I liked. Really liked. He was a handsome young man, not much more than twenty, wearing a long black coat that flowed down below his knee. He was clean-shaven, quite thin in the face, a strong scent of aftershave off him. A masculine scent. I could have stayed looking at him a bit longer ... but then I thought of the kids.

'You're delaying me now,' I say, trying to sound like I don't mind and getting ready to pass him by, after tearing myself away for a second from his mesmerising, piercing gaze.

'So what have you got in the bag here?' he asked

abruptly, as if he'd only just noticed it. He reached a hand out and took hold of it.

'Things from the shop,' I said thinking to myself that it was none of his bloody business anyway. For a very long second we both kept our grip on the flimsy handle of the bag ...

'Show me,' he said, glaring at me.

'What do you mean "show me"? There's nothing in it only ...'

'I have to see with my own two eyes,' he said snatching the bag. I let him take it, thinking that maybe that would be enough for him, knowing that at least there were no drugs in it, nothing illegal that I could be prosecuted over – and that he wasn't really out to mug me. Maybe he was looking for cigarettes, I thought, mentally making excuses for him, though I don't smoke myself and there were no cigarettes in the bag because I wouldn't please the wife by buying them for her ... But he wasn't to know that.

'I'm not looking for smokes,' he said, 'I gave them up a fortnight ago – the patch, it's a great help. Do you want to see it?' He was about to roll up his sleeve to show me. I shook my head, feeling shy for some reason.

'I only want to know what you have in here,' he said, peering into the plastic bag that he had pulled open already. He put it down on the tarmac in the middle of the road ... if a car comes, I thought ...

He started emptying it out eagerly, as if he was hunting for something in particular ... tea, sugar, milk, a bottle of Coke, firelighters, sausages ...

'You have toilet paper here,' he said, taking out two rolls of it. I told him then in no uncertain terms that I knew very well what I had in the bag, because everything in that bag I had taken off the shelf in the shop and put into it, except for the inside of the bag itself. I suppose I sounded fairly annoyed. I had every reason to be, looking down at the stuff scattered all over the place.

'So I'll thank you to tell me something I don't already know,' I say.

'Okay,' he said, cocky as you like. 'I'm hungry – now that's something you didn't know!'

'Well, knowing that won't exactly enrich my life,' I say.

'All right then,' he said. 'You're hungry too and what's in this bag here won't satisfy you.'

I made a face.

'And I'm going to start eating right now,' he said, tearing the paper off the sausages in one long strip.

'They're not yours!' I say.

'I'm only going to eat them,' he said, as if he was going to be able to give them back to me afterwards.

I snatched them off him, putting them behind my back with one hand, like a little boy who wouldn't share his sweets. He still had the plastic wrapper in his hand, twisted around his fingers.

'Keep them then,' he said, 'if that's the way you want it, and shove them up your arse.'

'There's no need to be so bad-mannered on top of everything else,' I say.

'I beg your pardon,' he said, 'but it wasn't the sausages I was going to eat anyway, but this wrapper.' And he stuffed the plastic into his mouth and started chewing ... honest to God. A car with a stranger in it went by on the other side of the road. It didn't stop.

What am I going to do now? I said to myself, hardly able to breathe while I watched him. Down he went on his two knees in the middle of the road. He blessed himself. He said a quick grace before meals, or some sort of murmur anyhow. Scared now, I let him go ahead. I won't have to carry them home to that madwoman anyway, I said to myself ... except that the kids will be getting impatient for the Coke.

He ate the toilet paper in long strips. He threw the cake out on the road and gobbled the box, tearing it into pieces with his teeth. He poured the salt out, unluckily, around his knees and stuffed the container in his mouth. He tore the box of firelighters into two pieces so that they all fell out on the road in a heap at my feet. He started guzzling them as if they were a packet of Mikados or Kimberleys ...

God, there's a man with an appetite, I said to myself. I took one step back from him with the shock of it. I had leather shoes on. New shiny, eye-catching leather shoes. He looked up at me from his knees, as if he was praying to me, imploring.

'Glass is my favourite, even though it has a sharp taste,' he said, breaking the bottle of Coke on a stone that was sticking up through the rough surface of the road, the liquid fizzing out noisily and spattering in fragrant bubbles all over the place until it had soaked away into the tarmac. I thought of the kids ... destined to go thirsty it seemed, poor little things. What was I going to say to them later? He picked up the silver bottle-top and chomped it as if it were delicious chewing gum, and then started on the little bits of glass left on the road. You'd think he was eating crisps the way he crunched the sharp pieces between his teeth. Afterwards I heard them fall down into his stomach, smashing against each other like a pane breaking ...

My ulcer.

'I eat anything and everything,' he said, 'and I love hot food,' stuffing the last firelighter, which he had nearly overlooked a few seconds ago, greedily into his mouth.

'I can see that you do,' I say. 'You like a snack on your walk.' Especially when the grub's not your own, I thought to myself.

'Oh, I always have a great appetite,' he agreed.

I said nothing for a scary moment. I heard the last bits of glass clink against each other somewhere deep in his stomach – like they were being processed in his gut.

'Do you know something, I'm still starving,' he said sounding quite upset. I looked at the low wall of grey stones and an iron gate beside me – a brand new iron gate, though it was showing a bit of rust already from the rain. I thought about how iron is good for the body.

'I wouldn't touch it,' he said, getting up from his knees and brushing a sprinkling of sand off his trousers and black coat. 'Can you not see the red 'No Trespassing' notice stuck up on the wall there beside you?' Sure enough there was a notice there. 'That wouldn't suit my purpose at all.'

'But I suit you, I suppose, me and my poor groceries,' I said warily. I looked at my watch, letting him know I was in a hurry. I was very late now. His stomach gave a noisy rumble.

'Do you not hear my guts knocking together with the hunger?' he said. I certainly could hear his innards complaining. An odd anxiety came over me. My new shoes, my trousers, my belt, the buckle … the zip of my trousers would be a delicacy. I'd better run – bad leg or no bad leg – or I'd be going home in my birthday suit, in front of everyone. And they'd all blame me.

'The environment as well,' he came out with the words suddenly, as if he was trying to interrupt my stream of thought.

'The environment?' I say. I wanted to look around me, but I didn't. I couldn't bring myself to take my eyes off him. Just in case.

'Yeah, the environment, now you have it,' he said. 'It'll have to be saved before it's too late. Right away.'

'Saved?' I say.

'Exactly,' he said. 'What do you think I'm doing here?'

I gave a screech of laughter. I had to. To convince myself I wasn't afraid maybe.

'So you're going to save the environment ... God bless you!' I shouted, relieved that he himself had changed the subject. It's a wonder he wasn't peering down from a tree like a bird or sliming up out of a tunnel in the ground like a worm if that was the case, I thought. But maybe I shouldn't be making a laugh of him all the same. Maybe it was a mistake. He looked so sure of himself.

'Recycling,' he said then. 'Recycling, just like people. Things have to be recycled.'

'People ... Things?' I say.

'Yeah, things, all kinds of everything ... iron, steel, paper, glass, clay ... from now on everything has to be recycled.'

My nervousness came back with a vengeance.

'Sure won't death and decay recycle everything and everyone in their own good time?' I say, defensively.

'Oh, we can't wait for that,' he said quickly. 'Have to hurry. Hurry. People can't wait. Recycle them all regularly, that's the way it has to be from now on.'

'Put an end to them?' I say.

'Give them a new life!' he says.

I thought then that I understood what he had in mind. I wasn't sure, though, if I could believe the half of what he was on about ... On the other hand there were two or three fellows about the place that I'd never got on with. What if I mentioned their names nice and quietly to him. And then there was my wife ... I felt a kind of giddy, merry puff of anticipation.

'And you're going to eat –'

'Now you're talking with your mouth moving,' he said, interrupting me, bursting to talk, not letting me finish my sentence. 'I couldn't wait to hear you say it yourself. And since you did, I'll start with you.'

'With me?'

'Yes. With you!'

'With me!' My eyes were glued to his face – to his mouth, his lips, his sharp teeth. 'But I'm a nice person,' I say, assertively.

'But sure the nice people are the nicest of all,' he came back at me.

'But I've almost made it to fifty,' I begged. My friends were organising a party for me the following week.

'What does that matter?'

'But it wouldn't be right.'

'Right? How would it not be right?'

'It would be unfair.'

'Nothing is right or wrong or unfair any more, if half of what I hear is true,' he shouted. 'Am I not what you want, or will you just not admit it?' He bent down and took my foot between his teeth, and gulped down my shoe in one bite, the lace trailing out of his mouth like a scapular as he chewed. He had a hell of a bite. Maybe if I was nice to him, I thought.

'And if I let you eat me up now, will I have done my bit?' I asked him, coming over all innocent.

'Your bit ...?'

'Yes, my bit,' I say. 'My bit for the cause, whatever the cause is ... the environment, the rainforests, the sea, society, the whales, oh yes, and the big hole in the ozone that's getting bigger every day.' Saying to myself that I might as well throw that in as well since everyone seems to be worrying about it these days.

'Indeed you will,' he said, pleased. 'By God you will. Now you're getting it, seeing how you can do the right thing for yourself, for the human race, for the world, God bless you. Recycling. People. Freedom.'

He took the end of my bad leg off in one big snap. I'd almost forgotten it and the pain in it until then anyway. The old pain wasn't there anymore, of course, but there was a different little ache in the stump that was left from the edge of his bite.

'It won't take me a minute to finish you off perfectly, if you'll just stay nice and still for me,' says he, his cheeks puffed out with the flesh of my leg.

'It's bad manners to talk with your mouth full,' I say, thinking of what my mother taught me when I was a boy.

'I beg your pardon,' he said, 'but you'll have to forgive me for that because I never had a mother since I was born, nor a father since I was conceived.' He bit off the end of the other leg, and I fell on my back on the road, legless.

'But what will happen to my wife and my poor kids when you've gobbled me up?' I asked him, realising now that I'd never see my legs again.

'Your wife!'

'Yes, my wife.'

'Huh. Sure didn't she eat the head off you this morning?'

'Well what about my kids then?' I, or whatever was left of me, asked again.

'What about them?' he said. 'Sure won't they make their own way when the time comes, just like ourselves,' he said, making a beeline for my heart.

Translated by Katherine Duffy

SOMETHING ELSE

I didn't want a new house, anyway. Or an old house refurbished. Wasn't my own lovely apartment as good as any house? I was proud of it. It was spick and span. Beautifully decorated. Nicely located in an area southwest of the city. A quiet area. An apartment with a compact kitchen, a spacious sitting room, a toilet, as well as a bathroom and two bedrooms upstairs. My own room, the master bedroom, with its remarkable panoramic sea view, and the other room, the one that was seldom in use, was quite big as well, and quieter because it was at the back of the house. So why would I want a new house ...?

'This house is a steal. You'll see,' he said. 'It's beautiful. You could say it's new, really, as it's only five years old. An old couple lived in it after they retired. No child has ever set foot in it. The carpets are as clean and new as if they were put down yesterday. Some of them have barely been walked on twice in a row!'

'But sure I'm just out for a walk,' I said truthfully, when I saw him standing at the door of the house. 'Just taking a stroll and passing the time!' He looked a bit impatient. A bit fidgety. There was a 'For Sale' sign at the gate and on a cardboard notice in one of the two front windows, and for some reason I acknowledged him, nodding in his direction. Out of courtesy, I suppose. I greeted him. Mentioned the weather. And we had a little bit of a chat after that and soon we were deep in conversation ... Strange, the ways people meet.

Suddenly he pushed up the sleeves of his jacket and glanced at his gold watch and braced himself. 'There's no chance this lot are going to come now,' he said. 'They were to have been here at eleven. It's after twelve now. They've completely wasted my morning.'

I realised then that he was an estate agent, killing time at the door of the house. 'Why don't you come in,' he said, 'and see what you think of the house.'

He was quite young, maybe about twenty-eight. Wearing a suit and a blue tie. Clean-shaven, neat and tidy. Clutching a black folder in one hand.

'I'll take a look at it,' I said, after a bit of thought, thinking I might as well since I hadn't anything better to do. I followed him in. He asked me what sort of place I had and what road it was on ... 'You'd have an extra bedroom in this house,' he said as soon as we were inside the door.

'I know I would, if I wanted it, that is,' I said, going on to explain that I'd have two empty rooms then which would only cause me more expense and hassle.

'But couldn't you let them out to lodgers, and make a few extra bob,' he said, 'with this city overflowing with students and tourists and what not?'

'Too much trouble for the likes of me,' I said, 'having to sort out things like that. And you wouldn't know who you're taking in under your roof, the way the world is nowadays.'

'But if you have a few euros put away,' he said, 'you couldn't do better than a little investment. Take this house for example ... Don't you know the way house prices are going in this city? Flying up by the week. By the day. Everything's going up.'

He was still standing in the big glass porch. Stained glass. A porch whose lower half was painted light blue. He put the folder that was under his arm down on the little table beside the front door. He took off his jacket and put it on the back of a chair.

'The heat comes on regularly during the day in this house,' he said. 'Of course it's needed at this time of the year, and with the house being empty. You can take your coat off if you like,' he said. I noticed the blue of his shirt, now that I could see all of it. A blue that was much softer than the sharp blue of his suit.

I saw that he was wearing braces. Braces must be back in fashion again, I said to myself. I always preferred belts ever since I was a lad. He hung my coat on the back of the door.

'Wait till you see the rest of the house,' he said. 'Wait till you see ...' and he stopped in the middle of the sentence and jerked his head, motioning me to follow him.

'This is the sitting room,' he said. 'It has great space.' And it had. A big sofa and fine chairs. Cream walls with a frieze. You could see looking at the walls that they wouldn't need painting or anything, unless someone was really fussy about colours.

'Do you see this?' he asked, drawing my attention to the big, bright window. 'PVC throughout the house. You'd never have to spend time or money on it.' He opened one of the windows for a minute. Took a deep breath, his chest expanding. Then exhaled again, watching me.

'Look at that view,' he said, steering me over to the great

panes of the window. 'Do you see that? Looking down over the city. You're right above it. At night the whole place below is lit up. White and yellow lights. But you don't get much noise up here, I guarantee you that. It's nicely tucked out of the way you see,' and I watched him looking out. He closed the window with his right hand.

'Wait till you see the dining room and kitchen,' he said, beckoning me to follow him. And they were lovely rooms too.

'Everything is included in the sale,' he said, gesturing emphatically at the big mahogany table made in an appealing old style and the six chairs lined up around it in the dining room. The table was spotless and smooth, so much so that you'd wonder if a hot plate had ever been set down on it. And, as he kept pointing out over and over, every piece of furniture was made of the finest wood.

'It's the same with these presses,' he said, opening one in the kitchen. 'As you can see, you have everything you need here. Fridge, cooker, a really nice sink, microwave oven. Dishwasher. Washing machine and tumble dryer.' They were all there. 'It was killing the family altogether that they weren't brought up here.'

'You live on your own, don't you?' he said, as a statement rather than a question. I thought he was thinking about the tumble dryer which he thought would be really handy for me. As if he'd know what would be handy for me, I said to myself. If he lived alone I imagined he was someone who didn't spend too much time in his house or flat. Then he ran a hand through his hair twice and stroked the top of his left ear with the same hand, as if it itched.

'If you want to come upstairs,' he said, 'I'll show you the bedrooms.'

'And there's a little extra toilet under the stairs there,' he said as we passed it. At the foot of the stairs he stood back politely to let me go ahead of him.

Why the blazes am I here? I asked myself. Why?

Up I went. It was a wooden staircase and I could hear his footsteps creak behind me at every step. I could sense him behind me, my hand on the polished banister to the left, thinking to myself that I had no need of this house or of any other new house. That the apartment I had was fine – even though it was attached to another apartment. Six of them altogether in the block. All I was doing was looking at this house by chance. All that had happened was that I'd gone out for a walk before starting to cook my dinner. I just happened to pass this house and take a momentary interest in the 'For Sale' sign that was at the gate. I had glanced at the house, the lovely front garden catching my eye, when I saw him standing at the door – the auctioneer or the estate agent ...

There was a wide landing at the top of the stairs. I stopped. To see which way to go, I suppose. He took two steps past me and opened the door to the right, the gold watch on his left wrist peeping from under the cuff of his shirt when he reached out. He wore a ring as well, but it wasn't a gold ring. And his hands were so white. And soft too, you'd imagine. The hands of an office worker ...

'Look at this lovely room,' he said. He walked in a semicircle around the room before sitting down nonchalantly on the bed. He adjusted the knot of his tie slightly. 'This room is very hot,' he said. And it was. 'It gets the sun, you see. Look how this room runs the whole width of the house,' he said. 'And look, there's a window on to the back as well.'

I followed him. 'Do you see the back garden down below there?' he said. 'There's great space in it and those walls make it very private. You could lie out there all summer sunbathing in the nude. If you wanted, you could do a bit of planting. Grow vegetables and things.'

'The garden's gone wild,' I say, for the sake of saying something.

'That's true,' he agreed. 'But as I said, it was an old couple who were living here and I suppose they weren't able to do much with it. Or maybe they didn't bother their heads about it. You know yourself …' And I did know. There was a silence for a while.

'In a way, you'd be the first owner, if you were to buy it,' he said then. 'The first real owner, you might say. You'd hardly think the old couple lived here at all.' He was smiling as he finished speaking. The sort of smile someone smiles when he's hoping to say the very thing you want to hear, at just the right time. I could see his torso in the dressing table mirror as he crossed from the back of the room.

'If you want to have a look at the other two bedrooms,' he said. 'They were never furnished, but they're decorated even so, painted and carpeted beautifully. In nicely matching shades of green, as you can see. You could turn one of them into an office or a workroom, if you wanted. Whatever would suit yourself, really.'

'What sort of price are we looking at anyway?' I asked, just to see how seriously he would take what I was saying.

I must have startled him a bit because he blushed slightly at first.

'They're asking four hundred thousand euro,' he said then, seeming to swallow hard at the same time.

'Four hundred thousand euro,' he said again and I saw a glint in his eye, and reckoned it was the mention of the money that might have sparked it …

'Of course I could put your own apartment on the market, and offset the value against it. I'm sure it would be worth well over a hundred thousand euro. If you want me to look at it, I'd be delighted. Any time.'

I kept an expression of uncertainty on my face as best I could as he was talking, although he was watching me closely. But estate agents are like that, I thought. All salespeople are like that. All sweetness and light, but watching all the time for the slightest little hint or giveaway sign in the faces of their quarry. Full of tactics and ruses, out for the kill. Almost without you realising it. He looked at his watch.

'I'm free now. Strike the iron while it's hot, as they say,' he said, laughing. 'If you're on for it, of course. I don't have to be back at the office until after lunch. I'll give you a price on the apartment at any rate. No harm in that.' He had an interesting smile on his face by now. Very interesting. There was another little pause. I began to smile too.

'As for this house, as I said, you couldn't go wrong the way the prices are rising in this area,' he said. He raised his arms in the air, illustrating his statement.

'But of course, you're welcome to get a second opinion anytime,' he said. 'You could get an engineer to look it over with you. Oh, I nearly forgot,' he said then. 'I nearly forgot to give you my number,' and he dipped his right hand into his little shirt pocket. I saw a small damp patch of sweat under his arm that I hadn't noticed until then. He took out two business cards at once that seemed to be stuck together.

He put one of them back in his pocket and held the other one out to me, turning it face up. I looked at it, mentally noting his name and the name of the firm he worked for. I didn't think it would be polite to read it out loud.

'We're based in Patrick Street,' he said, closing the bedroom door behind us. 'Oh, and here's another card with my mobile on it, my personal number. You can ring me anytime.'

'Certainly,' I said walking down the stairs ahead of him.

'And as you can see with your own two eyes,' he said, 'everything in this house is fantastic. Something else.'

It was he who was fantastic. Something else.

Translated by Katherine Duffy

No Room in Heaven

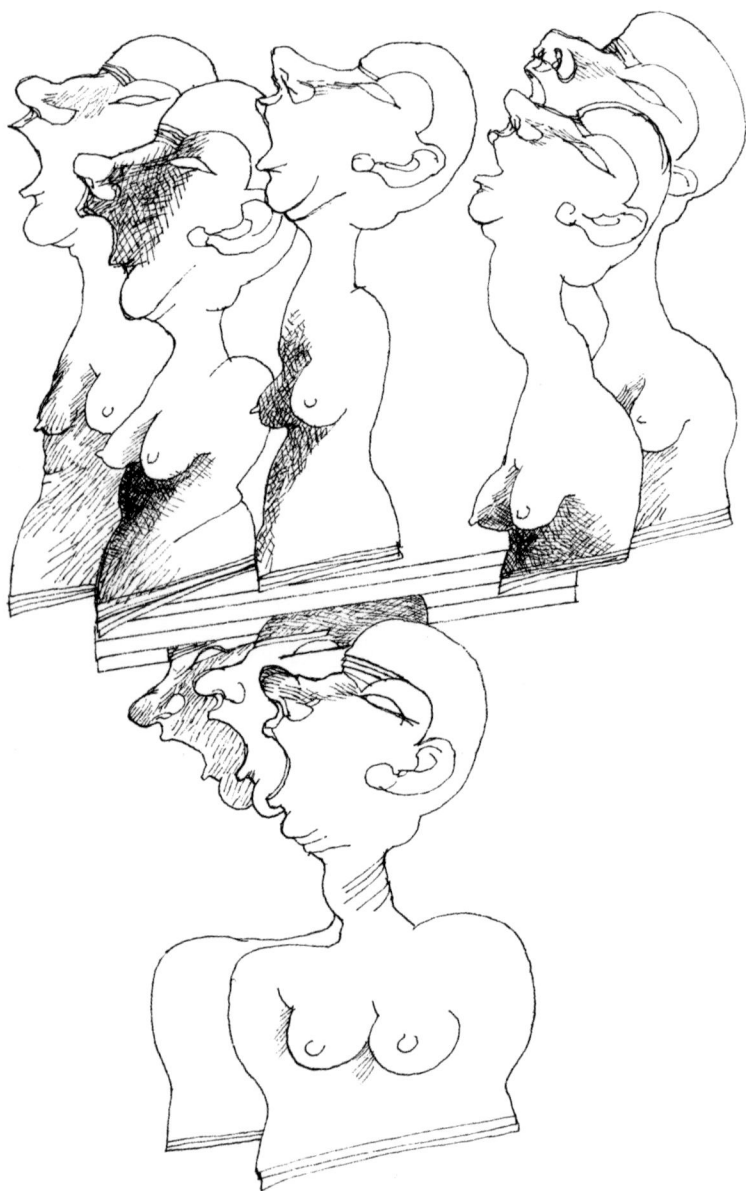

At the beginning of time God was greedy and kept every blessed thing for himself and his family. He would look down from on high at people scurrying here and there on the merciless surface of the earth, slaving away, trying to put food in their mouths to keep some glimmer in themselves of the life that he had forced upon them. They had no idea how to sow potatoes, rice, corn or vegetables, nor how to grow or harvest them because they had never seen seeds. God had them all stashed away. For himself and his family and friends.

They're all mine, he said. I'm the creator and I can do whatever I like, he thought. And he let the people go to hell, with nothing to eat but the wild berries that grew on trees and thorny bushes. Sometimes he wanted to burst out laughing to see all the scratching and scrabbling that went on below. He liked watching their antics as they shinned up tall trees and inched out on precarious branches, afterwards snatching the berries out of each other's mouths. The ones who couldn't climb – old people, children, people who had something wrong with them – there was nothing they could do but sit on the ground and wait, or else go crawling about, foraging for any scrap or shred of food that the ones up above might let fall, wolfing down any little bit of sustenance they could find.

One day God's daughter was taking a leisurely stroll

when she tripped on the root of a golden apple tree and went flying. As she was slowly getting to her feet she took a good look around her. That was when she noticed the people below for the first time.

'Oh Daddy,' she said, 'what are those?'

'They're people.'

'People? But what are ... people?'

'People! Human beings like them down there. What you see!'

'Oh! But look at the state of them. It's so sad.'

'Is it now?'

'We have thousands of different seeds here. We've more than two hundred kinds of potatoes ... banners, kerr's pinks, records ... more than a hundred kinds of rice, never mind all the other seeds. We're never hungry or cold, we want for nothing. Couldn't we share what we have here – or at least some of it – with them? Even throw down a few handfuls of seeds to make their lives a little bit easier?'

'Now there's a woman talking, if ever I heard one,' said God, taken aback. 'You take after your Mammy. I knew it from the very first day.'

What he was saying annoyed his daughter, especially the personal remarks, but she was clever enough not to let him see it. The last thing she wanted was trouble in paradise. She knew what her Daddy was like.

'But they're starving and desperate,' she said, 'and this place is overflowing. There are baskets of food sitting around, waiting to be thrown out after every meal. Even if they only got the crumbs that fall from our table.'

She looked down again at the people and saw how thin and wan and worn a lot of them were.

'The poor little things,' she said, knowing well that he was listening. 'Do the poor always have to be poor? For God's sake give them some seeds,' she begged again.

'They're alive and kicking, keeping body and soul together, aren't they?' God said. 'Has anyone of them died since time began?'

'I suppose not.' She allowed him that much. 'But they're very, very hungry!'

'Hungry! So what! I've said it before and I'll say it again. This is none of your business. Heaven's seeds are meant for heaven. If they eat them down there on earth, they'll die. They'll die, I'm telling you, do you hear what I'm saying? And if they die, then where will they go?'

Silence.

'Hah?' he said then when she didn't reply. 'I'm getting a headache from listening to you,' and he marched off into the house in a huff.

The daughter sat down heavily on a bare rock, not knowing what to do. He's never going to change his mind, she said to herself. What's the point in trying. Then her ears filled with a strange kind of music, a rasp of trumpets, as if the notes were resisting being played by their instrument, so that she wasn't sure if it really was music or just the wild ramblings of the wind. And since she had never heard music like this before she listened as closely as she could until the tune was played out. Then a long hush. She longed for the music. The longing deepened. Where does music hide when the tune is over, she asked herself. Where does it go when it leaves. Oh, where does it go ... what swallows it up ...?

She made her way back to the house, dragging her feet, still mulling over the sad situation those people were in. The music was a tangle of echoes still going around in her head. I'll lie down on my bed for a while and I'll think my thoughts and dream my dreams, she said, letting up the latch of the door quietly, because she didn't want any more arguments.

The snoring startled her. God was lying flat on his back on the bags of seeds, sucking and chugging the air and all that was in it, in and out through his nostrils. She saw at once that he was more deeply asleep than ever before, his snoring sending the midges and bees and butterflies into a whirl and slamming them to death against the window. Now's my chance, she murmured to herself, looking fondly at the seeds. He won't wake from that dead sleep anytime soon, she thought, noting the regular rise and fall of his big belly, like a bellows blowing the fire. She grabbed an empty bag and started throwing handfuls of seeds from the various sacks into it. She worked away happily until she had nearly filled it, and suddenly it burst. Not a single seed or grain was left, not even a stray one lodged in the rough fabric of the bag. She picked up another one, and another, but the same thing kept happening time after time – each bag burst and tore as if it was refusing to hold the seeds for her. Still she kept on for the rest of the day, until nightfall and long into the night. She sat down then and put her head in her hands in despair. She was beaten and she knew it.

'Don't cry now or you won't get to laugh later.'

The voice startled her. A Guardian Angel had flown down on to her breast and was whispering in her ear.

'Those sacks are trying to tell you something,' the angel said, 'because the seeds of heaven are no good on earth without a dose of heavenly water to fertilise them. Take what you can carry in your own body but leave your hands free for the rough journey ahead. And don't cry a tear or spill a drop of body fluid because you'll need a river of it later on. You'll need every drop of liquid you can spare.'

And with that, the Angel was gone. She jumped up and started tearing off her clothing, piece by piece, until she was down to the last two bits. Gracefully, she removed those as well. She went over to God and kissed him softly, carefully, lightly on the top of his head. Sweat from his scalp moistened her lips. Instinctively, she licked her lips, mixing the sweat with her own saliva. She swallowed the cocktail.

'This is it then,' she said to herself. She took a big, deep breath. 'This is it.'

She began raking up the seeds of the various grains and packing them as best she could into her ears, under the lids of her eyes, into her mouth and throat, up her nostrils, up her arse and into her crotch until her every crack, crevice and orifice was filled to the brim. Then she cleared out all the dust and lint that had been nestling in her navel and pressed a handful of seeds in there, hoping that they would stay put, glued by her sweat. She picked up her bundle of clothes and marched out of the house without a second glance, leaving the door open behind her. She gazed at the little earth below and almost got cold feet at the thought of the long, long way down. Her courage waned and was about to desert her when the day got brighter and once again she could see the people and the suffering they endured.

She closed her eyes and jumped down a little bit of the way. Then she took her hat and threw it on ahead of her and jumped another stretch. After that she threw her coat, her jumper, her jeans and so on, and for each piece of clothing she made another sprint along the way. At one point she got scared that she'd be left hanging between two worlds in a kind of limbo. But she kept going. She hurled her skirt on ahead and that spurred her on like a sail, her shoes, first one then the other, her socks and, when she got closer and the people could see her, she threw down her knickers, her belt, and finally her bikini, until she was so close to the earth's surface that she was able to jump down on to the summit of a high mountain, landing neatly on her tiptoes without breaking a single bone. She was exhausted after her journey and completely winded. Unable to stop herself, she rolled down the mountain, scattering seeds as she went. At the bottom of the valley she rolled to an abrupt halt. Waves of nausea and weakness washed over her and she threw up and voided everything that had been inside her. The people of the earth gathered around, amazed, but keeping a respectful distance at the same time. They didn't know who she was but they could see that this was no ordinary being.

'I came here for your sakes,' she sighed, as soon as she could get the words out. 'Against my father's will. To save your lives and to ease the hunger that's been gnawing at your insides all these years. From now on man will not live on wild berries alone. Let me do my work. Stand back a bit for now.' And she shed some big, salty tears. Then she started to squeeze out sweat from her face, her armpits, her navel. Spittle, drool and foam oozed from her mouth and, as she worked, snot and water flowed from her nose, piss from between her legs. Menstrual blood.

'Look at that,' someone said, 'she's suffering, giving her own blood.'

'For our sakes,' said someone else. 'For our sakes.'

The moistened seeds started to germinate. They sent out

shoots, put down roots. Buds broke. They grew. Potatoes. Corn. Rice. Vegetables. They grew and blossomed. And the people ate their fill. They got bigger. Stronger. Sounder. They fed. They thrived. They lived long, long, long healthy lives.

'When the swallows and the cuckoo arrive, it's time to start sowing,' she said. 'Springtime is planting time.'

And the people worked as hard as they could, doing exactly as she said, knowing that they would have a fortnight's food for every day they spent tilling the land and tending the seeds. Spring would lead to autumn's harvest.

All of a sudden one day one of them – an old man – died. This gave them such a fright. It had never happened before. His soul fluttered helplessly around his body, knowing it was in the wrong place but not knowing whether it should go east or west, down or up, because no other soul had previously left its body and gone before to blaze a trail.

'What's happening?' was the first question they asked God's daughter who was still lying there, a great fertile hulk on the ground. 'What's happening to us? We've never seen this kind of thing before? What caused this calamity? This death. You! It was you.'

When God woke up he saw his seeds had been raided and he went into a paroxysm of rage.

'This is her doing for sure,' he said, sitting up, then jumping to his feet.

'Oh the curse of not having a son,' he said, looking down at his daughter who was still busy irrigating the place with her water, her hot sweats, her cold sweats, her tears, one after the other, wringing every drop she could out of herself. She's really done it now, he said to himself, when he saw that acres and acres of the world's surface were covered with various seeds, each acre outdoing the next in abundance. People were lying around with pains in their stomachs from all they had eaten.

He ordered his daughter back up immediately and pushed her up against the wall. He tied her with ropes, bound her to a pillar and he whipped her and flogged her for all he was worth with leather belts and sea-rods for three days and three nights.

'Why did you betray me,' he asked, his voice breaking with rage.

His daughter was so weak she couldn't answer. After a while he untied the ropes that held her and she fell in a heap on the ground like a big sack of salt. He gave her a drink of brackish water that revived her a little and a few more drinks to give her strength because he wanted to hear the answers to his questions.

'Why did you betray me?' he asked again.

'A man's just died,' she gasped, 'and his spirit is caught between two worlds because he doesn't know where to go.'

'Oh really! Well isn't that just wonderful,' he said in a fury. 'And why do you think that is? It's because he's after eating the seeds of heaven that weren't ever meant for the earth. Death is in store for everyone now because of your disobedient meddling.'

'Because of me! But all I did was give them food,' she wept.

'Yes, you bloody fool, because of you and your misguided generosity. They would have lived forever down there if it wasn't for you! They might have been hungry but what did that matter? Now we'll have to share heaven with them! They can have your room, because you can rest assured they're not getting into mine!'

Translated by Katherine Duffy

LOST IN CONNEMARA

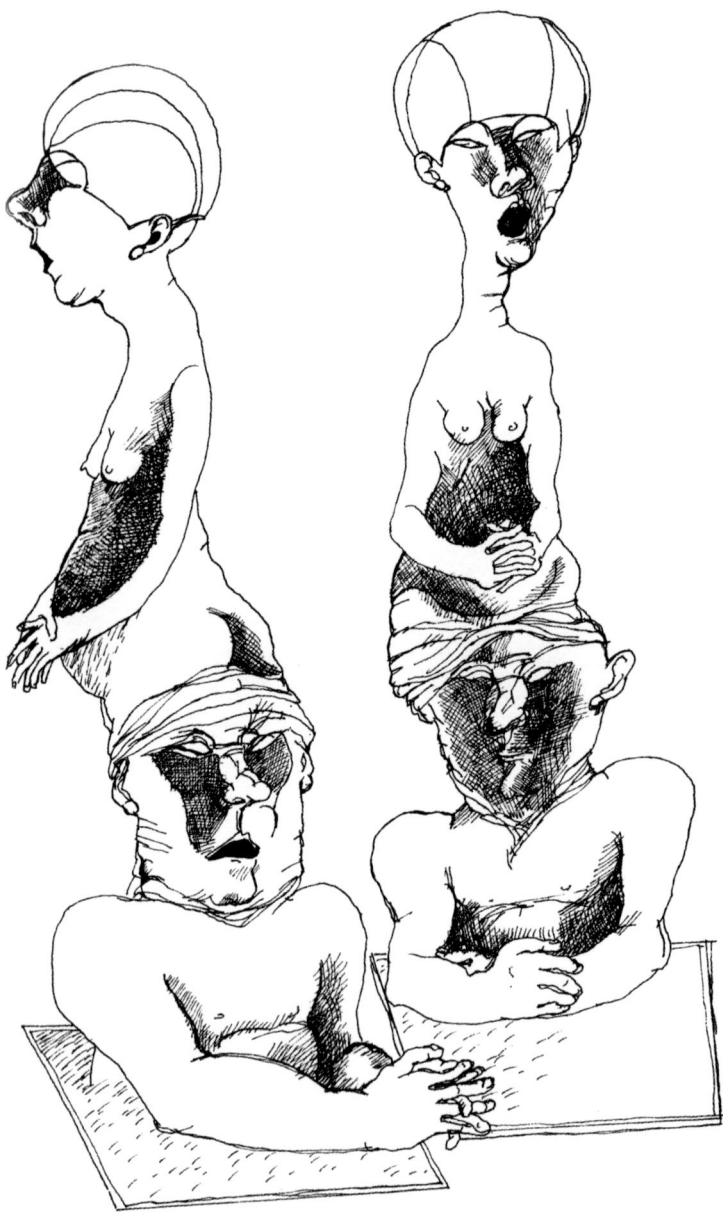

... I was lost in Connemara.

It was lack of sleep that drove me out so early. I didn't need a nagging alarm clock to wake. Wisps of sleep wouldn't come anywhere near me. They wouldn't give any shelter. They wouldn't smoother me or take me away from the pain, not even for a moment. I must have turned over two hundred times in bed. In between I lay on my back. Rolling into his side of the bed, leaving my own half deserted. Empty.

The sun was well up when I drew back the curtains at last, surrendering to daylight. There was a healthy freshness to the air when I stepped outside. Not a cloud in the blue sky. The sun rising steadily in the east. On its own. Ready to take command of the day. A superfluous moon in the west was backing off, kowtowing before it.

Off we went up the road. Silence reigned, except for the birds' chirpy twittering as they celebrated daybreak. Here and there a dog gave a lazy bark as we went past a house. Apart from that they didn't bother us. Never made a rush at us, or circled or trailed us, teeth bared.

I walked and walked and walked. Till we'd passed Ard an Bhaile and come on to the stony, muddy bog road that led on from the fork where the edges of the two townlands meet. Then on to the little winding path that snaked north off that, like a stray thread.

There birds were singing as loud as they could, making a great happy racket in this remote, isolated place. They had the whole place to themselves, almost. We were out in the wilderness now. The wild Connemara wilderness.

... Life is short, he used to say. As has often been said before. A relationship, any relationship runs its course, he used to say. That was before we knew anything for certain. Seize the moment, he'd say, before it seizes you. Take control. Seize the moment and draw it out to its full measure, like you would a coiled spring. Draw it out to its utmost, and hold it to that point as long as you can. That's all you can do, he'd say, with any life; good, bad or indifferent. On reflection, I'd agreed with him. He liked the image of the spring. I liked it too, now that I thought about it. The spring, rocketing you into the ether, lifting your heart and mind with one strong bounce. The energy, the intention in its coils.

I felt the soft bog shiver under me. Little tremors with my every heavy footstep. As if the wide, heathery surface of the bog itself was laid down on great endless rows of springs. No matter where I put my foot, there'd be another one underneath. But they were lifeless, pretend springs that only made it harder to walk. The effort of walking and the heat of the morning were bringing me out in a sweat, soaking my skin. Clusters of droplets gathered into big rolling drops that ran down my spine, tickling me. I took my shirt off carefully, throwing it over my shoulder like a tourist. There was no path here, not a trace of one. There were hummocks and hollows, hard ground and soft. The beauty of the purple heather growing thickly all around left me cold. It was like a huge uneven carpet with irregular patterns of flowers. Colourful as a rainbow. Every kind of wildflower showed its face here. And the bog cotton with its soft fibres. If there was enough of it I could make a bed to lie down on, I thought. But it would take an age to gather it all together.

The doctor we went to wasn't from the area. He was kind. Very kind. But how kind can kindness be? What good is it, after a certain point? It's positive I'm afraid, he said, speaking to him. And then he looked away, looked over at me. The two of us looked at each other. He was sorry, he said, very sorry. Stage three, he replied, when we asked the question together, like a line from a play that we'd rehearsed. About this time five years ago ...

I stopped at the mass rock. I wanted to have a rest in the glen here. It wasn't that I was tired exactly, but ... I sat down on one of the big wide stones to the right of the rock. It was nearly as wide as a double bed. Carefully, I set down beside me the jar that I'd been cradling up to now. I thought of how I'd come here the first time ever when I was a boy. The schoolteacher steering and shepherding us through the bog and the glens. We spent half the day here. Sixth class. Environmental studies. History class ... the time of the Penal Laws in Ireland, when Catholics were forbidden to practise their faith. Crowds would come to the masses that were said in secret here, in hiding, at irregular times, she explained. People were always at the ready to pass on the word. The priest disguised as a woman. I close my eyes for a minute. I imagine a huge crowd of people gathered around me. A pulse of nervous delight running through them at the thought of being able to hear holy mass. A healing relief at being able to practise and celebrate the forbidden spiritual side of their lives, together in secret. In deepest secrecy. Getting the better of the twisted, unjust English law, of the enemy.

... The little old gravelly voiced priest came to see us one day. Ten years or so ago now. Just a month before he was transferred abruptly from the parish to some monastery in the middle of nowhere. It was a Monday night, the night he used to go around visiting the old people, giving them holy communion and hearing confession. We'd been living together for six months or more at the time. He started by saying to me that he'd noticed I never came to mass anymore. Was there anything he could do for me? Did I need some advice? Was there anything I'd like to talk to him about? That was the excuse anyway. The reason he'd called. We. In a word, I said it. Us. Stressing the words defiantly, nodding towards my partner who stood, flamboyantly half-dressed in white clothes. I didn't mince my words. He exploded then, laid into me. All shook up and hostile and bitter. His eyes fixed on me as he gave his hoarse tirade. His gravelly voice breaking on a word here and there so that he ended up having to repeat whole sentences. Switching to English then, directing his talk past me, in through the door. As if the stranger, as he called him, spoke no Irish. Ye're a public disgrace, he yelled. A public disgrace to the village, to Connemara, to this country. A rotten example to the youngsters, to the people of the parish, to the teachings of almighty God. What would your poor parents say, the sweet blessing of God on their souls, if they were alive? If they knew the sort of carry-on going on under the very roof where they reared you as Christians? He stared deep into my eyes as if he could see my forefathers in them. Have you any respect for the word of God, for the gospel of the Holy Bible? There are nine ways at least, and more, of reading the Bible, I say, when I get a chance to speak, just like every other fairytale. Each to his own opinion, showing him the door. Ye'll pay for this, he said in that hoarse voice of his. Ye'll pay. Glancing sneakily in across the threshold. May the plague not pass ye by. Nor misfortune. How could ye have any luck? Ye'll be brought to the chapel yet, so ye will, even if ye're carried in on the shoulders of men, in ye'll come, feet first, whether ye like it or not ...

It's the space I come here for. That's what the two of us came here for, so often before. Expansive space. Freedom. Healing privacy and peace. The broad, endless sweep of Connemara. A limitless, unfettered sweep. Open, without boundaries. Not a fence or a moat or a ditch or a wire. Not a human pathway.

You could get lost here easily. Willingly even. A whole private world with a personal sky all of your own, wherever you stand. And I feel a deep connection with the bog that shifts beneath me with every step. A kinship. The marshy bits I jump across; the bare wide hard rocks that break its surface; the solitary grey stones that hardly ever feel the gaze of a human being; the mirror-like lakes where only wild animals or the birds of the air drink; the lonely green glens; the hardy cattle; the little hillocks and then the bigger hills that stretch away from me into the distance; the high, stately mountains, solid in the background beyond.

And this is where we came so often to walk in solitude, even after he got sick. It was balm for his heart, for both our hearts. Sitting here on one of these stones, we promised eternal love to each other. More than eight years ago. Nobody else would ever come between us, as long as we lived. We held each other tightly in the yellow twilight of autumn. The red sky a rounded, limitless open roof above us. Grey rocks and green stones under their living crust of lichen, like silent witnesses, participants, all around us. Approving our kisses. We slid down off the stone then, sank into a ready-made bed of wild grass. Where we celebrated the sacrament of our love, drank from the chalices of our bodies ...

I pick a flower. Just as we did that day. I even smell the same scent from it when I put my nose to it, a scent that erases, in a breath, the eight years that have gone by. It takes me back in one burst of fragrance to that glorious evening. I take out the jar which is in a cloth pouch attached to my belt. Picturing myself for a minute as a soldier or a hitchhiker with my canteen of water on a hot day, I lift the urn shakily to my mouth, and kiss the glass. I feel the little flush of heat that has built up in it from sunlight going through the light fabric of the bag. I stare at the grey ash ...

I was so near to him. Just thin glass between us. So little of him there, after all the life that was in him. Barely enough to set one wild flower growing in poor, barren Connemara soil. My right hand was still trembling as I twisted the lid of the jar, my eyes clouding over. I put my nose to it as soon as I had it open. I couldn't smell a thing. I let the tear that had run down my cheek fall right into it. Just as my tears had fallen on his breast so often before. But then I could see them after they fell. Could wipe them away. Dry them. I tried to recreate his face in the light mixture of ashes. Tried and tried, but I couldn't manage it.

This is it then, I said to him, to myself. I raised my head

for a minute. I looked to the southeast where the sun was climbing, heading for the centre of the sky. Then I stood at the top of the stone, or at least where I reckoned it to be. I gave the jar a gentle shake, so that some smooth, soft grains of ash tipped out, soft as talcum powder, apart from the occasional cindery fragment of bone that tumbled out with it.

I walked in an uneven ring around the stone. Anti-clockwise, against the sun. Leaving the track of the ash pretty thin in places, so that I could complete the circle. A sort of broken ring. But the long wild grass seemed to take it in, spirit it out of sight, as if it belonged to it since the beginning of time, as if it was reclaiming its own. I left the empty jar in a little cleft below the head of the stone. A little glass memorial to you, I tell him. I looked around at the witnessing stones scattered about us. Looking not a day altered or older, it seemed, than they were that day eight years ago. Take good care of him now, I said to the stones, looking at each, one by one. You'd swear they were listening. One or two seemed to lean towards me, bowing. Let his spirit go free from this life, to make its journey onwards, I call back towards them, as I start to wander away into the wilderness.

I used to ring to talk to him whenever he was ill in the hospital. Twice a day sometimes. As well as visiting him regularly.

I close my eyes. I walk like a blind man, moving tentatively. I open them, just a little, every five steps or so, just to check where I'm putting my feet, and it looks like everything is getting dimmer. I strain to make his face appear one more time. To conjure him up from the depths of my mind. Knowing he's there somewhere, if only I can find him, if only I can put my finger on him, mentally. Sometimes I nearly manage to capture a full image of him, but mostly something is missing – his mouth, his eyes, his nose, his chin – it's so hard to get them all grouped in the one picture. Then he appears as he was a few days ago – the last time I saw him – his cold chalky face springing into my mind, as if of its own accord. His eyes closed, the way I had closed them. When I open my eyes again, I try to see his face in the heather, in the colours of the flowers, in the long grass, but all I see is my own face in the jaws of the stones and rocks, or in one of the little lakes ...

At least he died at home, I think, taking comfort in the thought. Just as we wanted. With me holding him. Cradling his head in my hand from time to time. He hadn't been able to speak for a good few days. He had fits of shivering. Often he was pouring with sweat. But there was a watery gleam in his eyes; he could open and close them slowly. I kept wiping the sweat away. I used to wet his mouth with a drop of cold water whenever I thought he needed it. The doctor had said quietly to me the day before, when he came out of the room, that there was a chance he could still hear, and to keep on talking to him. I did ... And I told him that I'd be all right, that everything would be all right. I said that, because I wanted it to be true. So I'd told him a lie for the first time ever, even if it was a white lie.

He passed away at five past four in the morning. I was glad that the drugs had seen to it that he wasn't in pain, that I'd had my arms around him and was stroking his hair. I took his pulse and felt the beats slowing. Slowing. Stopping. My own heart was beating harder. I pressed my mouth to his. Then ...

I gave a sort of thanks to God a few minutes later, if you could call it thanks. I couldn't feel anything in my heart but there was a kind of knotty lump in my stomach. As for my mind ... I put out the light so that we were in darkness. I slipped into bed beside him and lay alongside him with my arms around him, between the damp sweat-soaked sheets. I pressed my cheek to his soft, damp cheek. I ran my hands gently over his warm body. I put my ear to his chest then, where I had heard the steady beat of his heart so often before now. The body was so quiet, so peaceful, so warm, so alive almost. I asked his soul to stay with me for a little while longer, told him I was in no hurry ... just one more hour ...

Let him go, I said abruptly to myself after a while. Let him go. I felt his spirit hover in the room. Set him free. His soul has a long journey ahead of it. His spirit wants to fly. Wants to be free, wants release from the clayey confines of the flesh. I drew back the curtains and opened the window. A breath of air from the western window met me. Just a gentle breeze, but it was still a wind from the west. Morning had broken but everything was still so quiet. Not a car on the road. No dogs barking. Not even the birds singing just yet. Take him with you, I say to the daybreak and to the spirits I sensed were at the window, waiting to carry him off. I looked back at the mound of his body still cosy in the bed. He's free, I say, out loud. Free from all harm. Soon I'd start work, laying out his body ..., while all of Connemara slept ... except for me.

It took me a while to get back to the stone. I needed a rest by then. I was shattered, completely exhausted. The sultry, unnatural heat had left me weak. I felt as if it was sucking all the moisture and life out of my body. My legs were buckling under me. It was a weary day in a weary life. I lie back on the stone, closing my eyes tightly, determinedly. The lichen and moss make a thin mattress under me. His face, I still can't recall it.

The faces of other people flit across my mind far more readily without my trying to recall them at all. Faces of people I don't know half as well and have no wish to see or remember right now. Some of them belong to the small group of friends who came to the little ceremony we had. A warm, caring group, like a family gathered for a christening, not like the unfriendly crowd you get at weddings, watching and weighing everyone up. One of the faces is someone who sang a song. Was someone ... but even that face has faded again. They're saying things that sound like prayers.

They're saying the prayers in two parts. I hear them. The same voices answering ... the rhythms ... the sounds ... echoing back. Somehow I don't see the point of some of these prayers. Wouldn't you say it's someone else they're praying for? Wouldn't you think they'd suit some other occasion better? There's one short prayer that nobody makes the response to. Maybe there's no response to it, or maybe the prayer itself has the response built into it. What use to me are these mismatched prayers? ...

And who are these people hurrying towards me now? Strangers. Strangers, no less, well they must be, since I don't know any of them from Adam. They're not from Connemara. Two men and two women, fairly young at that. Well the cheek of them, doesn't it just beat all. Can't they see this is a private occasion? I hadn't put a notice in the paper or anything. The man in front approaches me. They're tourists right enough, he says. Germans. He's speaking in broken English. He shakes hands as if he's congratulating me. He wants to go to the Aran Islands, he says. Today. Wants to know where they could get a boat. Rossaveal, I say. The pier in Rossaveal. The morning boat would be gone by now, I tell him, but he might get a flight if it's urgent, depending on whether there are seats left or not. I point southwest to the airport. He shakes his head, disappointed, saying the other man's wife is afraid of flying. *Muise*, is that so, I say, but it's only nine or ten minutes and the planes are safe. He asks me what am I doing here? I tell him. He offers his condolences, congratulating me at the same time. Thank you, I say, twice, and he explains my situation to his companions, who stand a few feet away. One of the women immediately starts crying and the second one tries to comfort her. The woman who isn't crying says she'd like to stay with us, that the Aran islands will still be there tomorrow, that they're archaeologists trying to date a body that's been found there, but that they can do all that another day. After all one more day is nothing to a body that's been dead for thousands of years, the other woman says through her tears. Thank you, I say. The more the merrier.

A sudden shower of rain startled me awake. For a second, I wasn't sure where I was. Cold drops sliding down my face. When I opened my eyes and managed to focus again, it looked like the dark sky was bulking up and closing in on me, pressing down as if crushing me against the stone, which was hard beneath me. Extremely hard. Its lumps and bumps had dug into my skin and it felt now as if they had pierced sharp little holes in it. I peeled myself up and away from it. I felt a huge emptiness in my stomach, and I reckoned it was that that had actually woken me. A bottomless hollow. The stabbing hunger was twisting my guts into knots. I hadn't eaten a thing that morning. Couldn't face food. For the last month or so I hadn't been eating well. I went to look at my watch, and realised it wasn't there, I hadn't put it on that morning. But I knew from the ominous sky that it was getting late. At first I thought I was going to faint, but then I realised it was just a bit of dizziness. Probably from sitting up, then standing up too suddenly. I sat down. The raindrops were gathering force, getting heavy now.

Looking up, fully awake by now, I saw that the menacing heavens were about to open. I'm in Connemara anyway, I thought, wherever else I might have thought I was. That's for sure, and getting seven kinds of weather in the one blessed day. Run. But what use would that be? Where would I run to anyway with no shelter anywhere within an asses roar of me on this wild, flat land where I was marooned. Not even one gnarled, blanched bush itself.

I knew I couldn't run anyway, not while I was so weak and hungry. I just wouldn't be able. I stood up. My left leg gave way under me. I nearly fainted. I sat down again. Cramps shot like arrows down the leg. My stomach was stuck to my back with the hunger. I began to wonder if there were grains of ash under my feet. My heart contracted in my chest. Tears welled up in my eyes. I looked down again. I saw myself then as someone sitting in the debris of his house after a raging tornado has passed. Is this it, I asked myself, stretching my arms out. I look up at the gloomy sky. The rain falling sharp as shoemaker's knives. Wetting me. My back. My buttocks. My waist, under my belt. You'd think it was washing my face, washing my tears away. Trying to help. Rinsing the salt from my cheeks. Who gave this rain the signal to fall, I wonder? Did he send it to wipe away my tears?

But I'm wet. Drenched. By the time there's a short break in the weather I'm soaked to the skin. My clothes stuck to me like hard, cold plaster. It feels as if half my body's trapped in plaster. Cold spiralling up through me. Up my spine. Shivers. I wipe the drops off my face one more time. I slick my hair back, squeezing the excess water out of it. Although the sky is clear, darkness is creeping up, pressing its affections on the craggy lonely terrain all around me. The time. I'm about to look at my watch again ... but a blind man could see night is falling. At least this darkness seems to me to be more natural, more sympathetic than the cloudy, annulling darkness of the rain. Gradually it is stacking little friendly shadows up around me. I don't feel the cold and the wet so badly anymore. Or maybe it's that I've got used to it, or maybe I'm just drained of all feeling.

But I'll stay here with him a little while longer. I'll stay here on the smooth bog until night zooms in on me completely. So I'm nearer to him. Maybe I won't feel the void so much when night packs itself in soft blocks around me. Maybe I won't feel the desperate space that's widening all the time. The same airy space that used to draw us here for our long walks, when we were both under the one bright sky ...

And I look deep into the black sky again. To see if I can find his face in the twilight, or if the dark colours will shadow it on the sky of my mind. But I can't see, even though I studied the big picture in the sitting room for ages before leaving the house this morning, so that I could take his face with me ... wherever I went.

Night falls on me. Slowly. Surely. Darkness pouring down, wrapping itself around me ... A half-moon appears in the sky to the east, giving out a jot of light. Or is it to the west? The stars come out for me, one by one, and soon there are millions of them. Conspiring to make a glittering canopy over my head. Like sequins shining in a curve of deep thick carpet, one you could run your fingers through, you'd imagine, if you could only reach it. But you can't. And in that smiling, starry sky I can't find his face. Even though it's filled with living, shining eyes. I trip and bang my knee on the end of the stone, and this brings back to me how damp and cold my clothes are. I try to say a prayer for his soul. I wind my fingers into the coarse, wild, wet grass trying to find a trace of the circle of ashes. Some few of the grains. But the zealous rain has washed it all away, long before now. It's been swallowed up by the land. The rough, barren, mountainy land. Common land. He's lost to this hungry ground, is what I'm thinking, down on my knees. And I can't get hold of even as much of him as would blacken the nails of my wet fingers.

I craned my neck to take in the clear starry sky one more time. I felt the stars come closer to me. Closer and closer as if they were sifting downwards in a great scattering on top of me, down on to the countryside, down over all of Connemara. Soft blunt arrows. Soon I'd try to make my erratic way home, I thought ...

He's yours now, I say up to the stars, staring till my eyes glaze over, scanning for one falling or sparking upward to heaven. But not one of them stirred to see me home, to keep me company, none to brighten my broken way.

Translated by Katherine Duffy

Acknowledgements

'Father' won the Hennessy Literary Award in 1997, and was previously published in the *Sunday Tribune*, the *Fourfront* anthology (Cló Iar-Chonnacht, 1999), *The New Picador Book of Irish Fiction* (Picador, 2000) and *The Hennessy Book of Irish Fiction* (New Island Books, 2000).

'Death at a Funeral', 'Seven Hundred Watches' and 'The Man Who Exploded' were first published in the *Fourfront* anthology (Cló Iar-Chonnacht, 1999).

'The Colours of Man' was first published in *The Literary Review*, vol. 40, no. 4, summer 1997 (Fairleigh Dickinson University, USA).

'With These Hands' was first published in *Honeysuckle, Honeyjuice: A Tribute to James Liddy*, edited by Michael S. Begnal (Arlen House, 2006).

'The Mercyfucker' was first published in *Gay Community News*, October 1997.

'Lost in Connemara' was first published in *Irish Pages*, vol. 3, no. 2.

'Whatever I Liked' was first published in *Twisted Truths: Stories from the Irish* (Cló Iar-Chonnacht, 2011)